HEART BEATS YOUR NAME:

VOWS FROM THE BEYOND

BOOK FOUR OF THE *KASTEEL VREDERIC* SERIES

*"In life or even in death, you be only mine.
Immortally I give you my oath, I shall only be
yours."*

Ann Marie Ruby

DEDICATION

ONLY A HEARTBEAT

"The voyage of life ends as the path ends. Yet the melody of true lovers never ends as they call upon one another like nightingales even beyond death."

Life is only a heartbeat away from death. However, that never prevents twin flames from falling in love. That never prevents a mother from loving her child eternally. Or a child from loving a mother infinitely.

Dedication they have for one another is not just throughout one life but eternally. The lover's lane is always filled up with travelers and their eternal love songs keep the lane alive throughout time. As long as there is love, there is life, and as long as there is life, there are lovers traveling through the lover's lane of life.

There are family members who become a walking support for one another. A traveler can travel alone on a lonely road. Yet life becomes a joy when there is someone who is walking by your side like the white cane of a blind person, or the blessed hands of a mother or a beloved who never lets you fall.

I believe love never fades away nor blows out like a candle within a windy stormy night. The magical lanterns of all lovers guide twin flames to one another through life or even in death. Love keeps the bond of families eternally as the tree of life keeps growing.

For what is death? Is it not just the end of the earthly heartbeats? For true twin flames' hearts beat for one another even beyond time.

What about a mother? Could she not hear your heartbeats? Or a father? How could he not hear the heartbeats of a child?

Twin flames rise again and again like the rising phoenix from burning ashes to be with one another over and over again. The vow of, "Only for you I shall rise, even beyond death" keeps them bonded with one another throughout eternity. The vows of eternal twin flames have kept this Earth going throughout time.

Faith in true love is not a myth or a mystery unsolved but is a question and answer not found anywhere except within the inner souls of the beloveds. What about soul families? Are they not bound within the vows of a family throughout time?

I have sought this question over and over again as to why does my inner soul only seek him? Why does my heart beat only his name? I asked myself why do I love you my twin flame? I asked myself why do my mind, body, and soul only want you?

I realized dear twin flame, for you I am and without you, I am not. For you I want to have a family where our children too will learn to love. For you I would love to adopt all the children of this world into one home of love. Could I love all the children of this world? For you, would I rise like a phoenix over and over again?

All my answers were found within the simple word, love. I kept on saying for you my love, I live. These answers were not found within known knowledge. Still I believe the answers lie only within the inner souls of all twin flames.

I have given you all immortal, passionate love stories as my personal gifts to all twin flames and soul families. For all humans seeking their twin flames. For you who only wants a family. For you who is waiting to be adopted by a loving family. For you the lonely soul who dreams of one day, "I will find him." For you who needs to renew your faith in twin flames and soul families.

Today I bring upon you yet another immortal, passionate love story to awaken your faith in twin flames. For all of you I have created Kasteel Vrederic. There you will find a soul family, which throughout time has been there for one another throughout life and yes, even beyond death.

This book may be fictional. Nevertheless through the fictional characters, you too will be able to dream about your twin flame. Dream about being a part of a soul family which is there for you even beyond time.

For remember a dream can come true, only when you make it your destination. So today come travel with me,

iv

while I teach you how to dream a little. Come journey through a paranormal love story where I bring in the question of what if twin flames were separated by a breath?

Would they stop loving one another? Would they create a bridge through faith and belief in one another, even if that means they must go against all the known knowledge of this world? Would twin flames call upon one another through the door of dreams?

What about a mother's call? What about a father's call? Would a dead child return to his parents through the doors of dreams and reincarnation?

My answer is why not? Even if just for a while we could travel through the minds of what if, let us then travel through the doors of only eternal love and belief. Do you love your twin flame only while his or her heart still beats, or even beyond?

If your answer is beyond, then travel with me through the pages of this book. It is then you too will realize why I have dedicated my faith to twin flames, as from this blessed union we have families and the society is then born. Yet twin flames shall always rise even beyond time.

Come travel with me through the pages of a fictional romance story where I show you how to fall in love again. "Love and falling in love with you," the phrase in itself is so deep and romantic, it's better to fall in love than not see love at all. So why not fall in love with him in your dreams? Why not hold on to him and never let him go, even though it's only a dream? Tonight dream of your twin flame and tell him you love him eternally. At least then, you too have faithfully fallen in love with him and are faithful till the end of times only for him. Now my friends, no one can say you have not found love, for you have even though it's only in your dreams.

For my eternal belief in the concept of twin flames, I dedicate this immortal love story to eternal twin flames. If you too believe in true love and the power of twin flames, then come and say I shall never let you go for my,

Heart Beats Your Name: Vows From The Beyond.

TABLE OF CONTENTS

PROLOGUE

"The moon still shines even without you. The morning sun shines brightly at dawn even without you. How could you be sleeping so peacefully under the blue skies, your bed is the cold Earth, while I rest in bed sleepless?"

Antonius van Phillip watches the mountains from his Tennessee cottage in his dreams and sees his twin flame Katelijne Snaaijer in spirit form.

ll is quiet and nothing can be heard even though it is pouring outside. The soundproof windows and doors of this cottage can hide all the sounds of the outer world. Mother Nature's free musical concert tonight is hidden away from me. Gatlinburg, Tennessee in the United States of America is where I own a small cabin.

I hide within the Great Smoky Mountains range. This range is along the Tennessee and North Carolina border. The Great Smoky Mountains range was named after the miraculous blue mist that covers the mountains and always hangs around.

The visitors are seen vacationing in this mystical range. Wedding couples are trying to keep their memories alive within the cascading waterfalls. Tourists capture the wildlife roaming around on their cameras to take home and frame. A view that is compared to Heaven, stretches over five-hundred-thousand acres. I too had searched everywhere I could to get a small cabin in the woods, where I could be left alone. I wondered if I too lived near Heaven, maybe I could visit my family members whom I miss so much that living was becoming impossible but would be a little easier.

Maybe if I could pretend life does not exist beyond this cabin, it would be easier. Yet how could I stop hearing the heartbeats of my beloved family member whose heart does not even beat anymore? Was it his fate or my destiny? Or the journey of life that separated us by a breath?

Nonetheless, I never wanted to hide the outer world and all the musical sounds from me. Rather I wanted to hide away from the world. Here I found myself confined in a cabin where even the world was hidden away from me for the cabin was built soundproof as to my request.

I wondered if the world were closed up, then maybe my twin brother would be able to come back to me. I wanted the world to be totally dark yet I had the gift I carry with me always that had poured light back into my life. I never wanted to see, if it meant you had to close your eyes, as you left me with this gift.

My twin brother Andries van Phillip had passed away in Amsterdam, the Netherlands in a strange car accident exactly three years ago. Identical looking yet our pediatrician had said we were mirror twins. We had brown hair, brown eyes, and olive-colored skin. Both of us wanted to look like our elder brother so we grew French beards like him.

Our father was Dutch and our mother was of Italian origin. We did not get our Big Papa or our father's height as we were both six feet, two inches tall. My twin brother had a small black birthmark on his right shoulder and I have the identical one on my left shoulder.

All of my friends told me time would heal my inner pain, as time heals everything. Yet life froze like a deep-frozen lake and even to this day, my inner soul is frozen. My parents too died at a very young age when I was only a few months old. I was raised by my uncle and aunt, with my twin brother. My uncle and his wife never made us feel we were not their biological sons as they raised their only biological son, my elder brother, exactly the same way.

My big bro whom we both have always loved more than life was, is, and shall always be our admiration of love and kindness. Even though he is only two years older than us, he calls us his babies. My uncle had said our family members love to leave us alone as they one by one had gone to the other world. He jokes it must be a better vacation resort as they all rushed to get a free booking over there.

Like always, I was left behind. One minute younger I was than my twin brother, yet forever I was called the youngest and now dear brother, I am older as you have stopped aging at twenty-seven. My mirror twin brother gifted me sight by donating his eyes as I was blind from birth.

The accident that took his life and closed the door of light for him had gifted me with light. I dread this fact yet I cherish my brother's sight. For within my sight, you will always be with me through my eyes.

I was told by my very Dutch uncle, life is only a journey. We must finish this journey like the brave sixteenth-century soldier Theunis Peters, whose bloodline I carry. Even to this day, this brave soldier and his twin flame Griet van Jacobus, daughter of Jacobus van Vrederic, still guard our family home Kasteel Vrederic.

A huge portrait of the sacred couple still hangs in our library. The six-foot-tall soldier with long blond hair and blue eyes holds on to his beloved wife Griet, an enchanting woman with black hair that sparkles nearly blue like a raven's wings, with enchanting deep brown eyes, and olive-colored skin. She is embraced within the beloved arms of her beloved husband.

Now my brother who performed the surgery had taken a break from his world traveling. He had stayed with me at my Tennessee home to get me adjusted to the visions I was not born with. He is the only surgeon who had successfully completed a complete eye transplant surgery.

Whilst everything was dark for me from birth as the Creator had turned off the lights in my world, suddenly the lights were turned on in a dark world. I could see everything but my twin brother, yet my elder brother was my survival strength. His shoulders were my support where I had placed all of my weight upon.

My aunt and uncle too had come here to get me acquainted with my sight. It helped me forget the pain linked to it as my aunt is also my adopted mother who carries and buries all the pain within her chest and lightens all others around her. My uncle is my adopted father who took my twin brother and me into his chest when we were orphaned.

In our family, there were no cousins as we became a family through the bond of love. My aunt became my Big Mama and my uncle became my Big Papa, as they never wanted to erase my parents' names from existence. My Big Mama always says she carried her twin boys for two years. The story is my brother was a naughty child going through the terrible twos, whom Big Mama found easier to carry around. Because I was born blind, Big Mama was too scared to let me go, so she carried me around until she felt safe.

My elder brother, the only biological son of my Big Mama and Big Papa, had also performed another surgery three years ago in which he had transplanted my twin brother's heart into an unknown victim. Usually, these organ transplant receivers live only for a short period of time from less than one year to several decades. My brother is the first surgeon who was the first to discover and perform these transplant surgeries.

His message to all of us within the family is, live your life to the fullest and always believe in miracles. For even beyond doctors, there is always the door of miracles which opens for all only through knocking. Don't live your life in fear but live with faith.

We are the only successful patients who were told we would live a healthy life if we are given a healthy lifestyle. My brother is a miracle for this Earth as he is also researching on reincarnation and theories about dreams. I wonder if I should confide in my brother and tell him I am being haunted by a stranger ever since I survived the accident.

I wonder if my surgery had anything to do with my dreams. My brother had told me this surgery would be very complex and had a lot to do with the nervous system and connections. I had faith in my brother and my donor, my mirror twin's last wish. My twin brother's dying wish was for me to have sight. Yet, he on that day had gifted life to one other person I never got to meet, as typically donors and receivers never get to see one another and neither do their families.

I never had sight and never knew how it felt to see the world when you are awake. I know I could see in my dreams yet in the awakened state, it was all dark. Today the Tennessee mist and fog are not strangers for me. This was a miracle where I could adjust to the society slowly. A famous blind painter I became, since I was trained by the very persistent Dutch painter, my Big Papa.

Today I see an unknown face of a mesmerizing mystical princess, even when I am asleep. The spellbinding dreams started arriving ever since my surgery. One particular dream I see on a nonstop basis is so mesmerizing that I don't want to wake up. It is like the blue fog over the Great Smoky Mountains that mesmerizes everyone who sees it and never wants to go.

My beloved mystical princess, you know I can't sleep yet every time I try to close my eyes, I see you. I want to close my eyes just to see you but then you disappear. Yet I kept on having a strange dream on repeat for the last few years, I wonder why? This dream is as follows, my sweetheart, my beloved mystical princess of the night.

For you I write this in my diary. For I know you will read my diary sleeping next to me one day in my arms. Remember this diary too will go onto the bookshelves of the Kasteel Vrederic library for all future generations as my gift.

The dream is as follows, "I was seated in a gondola with you on my lap. You were asleep and I felt the Grim Reaper was trying to take you away to a faraway land. I had landed on the gondola to only hold on to you so you don't drift away. Then as I began to fall asleep, you were trying to slip away. It was then, I heard this amazing pianist playing a heartbeat sound on his piano as if trying to keep both of us awake. I tried to see who the amazing pianist was but only saw a baby boy playing like a professional pianist. He was playing the melodies of a sound that sounded like musical heartbeats."

My dream breaks at the first glimpse of dawn. I was a blind man who did not know the difference between day and night, until I was gifted with this blessed sight. It is strange to be able to witness the difference of this miracle with my sight.

Even though I do have the miraculous sight, I still don't see her in the daylight hours. I see her only in my dreams, during the dark nights when all are asleep and nothing can be heard except the nightingales who sing calling for one another. If all of this is not normal, or natural, then why am I being pulled toward her? Why does an unknown name and face come and awaken the inner heart of a lonely soul? I must confide in my kind and noble-hearted brother, Dr. Jacobus Vrederic van Phillip, if I get to see him any time soon. For he never stays in one place, as he travels around the globe at his own expense, performing surgeries for free.

I must tell him I have been haunted since my surgery by a strange female who keeps on repeating, "Wake up Antonius van Phillip, my heart beats your name, even beyond death."

I must confide I also see a child who keeps on calling me Papa. He keeps on repeating, "Papa, take me home. She is crying for me, my heart beats her name."

I wonder who is the child crying for? Who is he calling over and over again? I kept on thinking about all of this and could not get it out of my empty chest. Yet tonight I had stayed awake watching and admiring the Great Smoky Mountains range and the night skies.

Tonight, the moon was ever so bright with a mystical blue fog around her. I wondered about the sweet yet somewhat frightened voice of a very fragile-sounding woman. She calls me like a nightingale always to help her.

I wonder what kind of help would I be, as I am a blind man who just got his sight. Yet I still need a cane to help me or guide me around as it has become my life support. Now how could I be of any help to someone else?

Yet I will not refuse to help anyone as it's my noble duty for I am from the bloodline of a very noble man. Where do I find this helpless person? I must talk with my Big Mama who is a dream psychic and would know the answers I seek even before I ask her. She is my mother who did not give birth to me yet had raised me and knows when I need help before even I know of it. I know as I call upon my Big Mama, she will somehow know and call me before my thought ends.

Tonight I shall only dream of you my brown-haired and brown-eyed mystical princess. I can't tell your origin, but I can imagine you to be of heavenly origin. The caller of the night, peacefully sleeping in a bed that is soft like the skies. I will compare you to the ever-glowing moon in my book of unseen, unread poetry.

Oh my mystical princess, I don't know who you are as of yet, still I will write my love letters through poetry for only you. I will keep them in my daily diaries for you to read, as one day I believe you will be sleeping within my arms in my chest reading my love letters written in a poetry format only for you. My beloved, here is my first poem written with love only for you as I wait for you, sleepless.

My first poem for my love,
who sleeps like a mystical princess so
peacefully. Sleep tight my love and have
sweet dreams.

SLEEPLESS

Moon with her enchanting laugh
Shines upon the Earth for only us.
Everyone on Earth is asleep.
Nightingales are out singing
Sweet fragrant, romantic tunes.
The fervent wind too calmed down

As he too waits for her,

His darling pouring rain

To come and play with him.

Within the embrace of a lover,

Sleeps his cherished.

In the heavens above, sleep the stars

As they blink with drowsy eyes.

The moon glows as she dozes

Within the embrace of the night skies.

Tonight my pouring eyes see everything.

Tonight I realized the difference

Between day and night,

For tonight, I, a blind man, have sight.

Yet I watch the beautiful moon sleeping

Within the comfort of the heavenly skies.

Dear moon,

Tonight with this blessed sight,

I know you are the glowing hope

For all the lonely hearts.

So tonight, even though you are glowing

Ever so bright,

Pouring tears and the gripping pain

Of sadness force my eyes to be tonight,

SLEEPLESS.

Sleep well my dear caller of the night. I will find you and see you in the light. I will find the holder of the little pattering heartbeats, who ever so lovingly seeks his home and says, "Take me to her please, for my heart beats her name."

I shall never let both of you go, for I promise I shall find both of you. With the blessed sight, a gift from the beyond, I too continue my family tradition and this is my diary. I call my diary in the whispers of my sweet nightingale who so sweetly sings to me and says,

Heart Beats Your Name: Vows From The Beyond.

This is my diary and I am,

Antonius van Phillip

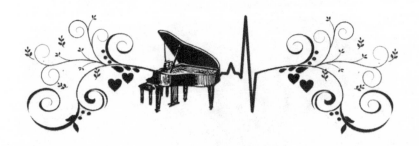

CHAPTER ONE:

Fortune Teller's Warning

"Destined to destiny we all are yet why then are we so frightened of knowing about our destination? Or could we by knowing the truth then change our destiny? For should we ignore all the psychics and the fortune teller's warning?"

Antonius van Phillip walking through Gatlinburg, Tennessee, keeping close to his heart the white cane his Big Mama had given him.

Tennessee welcomes the world travelers with open arms through her famous cities Chattanooga, Memphis, Nashville, and among other cities, my own hometown for the last few years, Gatlinburg. The voices from beyond still play musical notes in the air as Tennessee is the home of world-famous musicians such as Elvis Presley, whose musical melody "Love Me Tender" always sings sweet notes within my inner soul. Twenty minutes' drive from my own cabin is the famous theme park Dollywood, co-owned by the famous singer Dolly Parton.

The magical sounds of sweet voices spread throughout the Great Smoky Mountains and into my small cabin in Gatlinburg. Sweet voices singing the immortal musical notes relax my mind. My heartbeats can actually feel the romantic pull of the miraculous voices, as they give me hope that love is immortal like the sweet songs of the night.

Yet even my tired restless body can't sleep. Sleep left me as I awakened with sight. The one person I had so wanted to see when I had opened my eyes, has left me with the gift of sight. Yet he has gone to a place where I can't even give him a call and listen to his screams or follow my sense and find him waiting for me at all times.

Never had he left my side as he worried I would bump into something and fall. He always made me laugh as I would bump into things because I could not see, yet he would bump into everything because his hair was shoulder length, and mine was always cut short. Big Mama would be able to differentiate between us through our hair.

Even though I always had my dark glasses on, later on I realized my brother too had worn dark glasses all the time. I wonder, does he not worry anymore? For then how could he be somewhere I can't even see with my sight?

My brother Andries had given me the miracle of sight. As he laid in the hospital bed taking his last breath, he had asked our elder brother Jacobus to do this favor and perform one of the first transplant surgeries to be recorded on Earth as a success. Andries had said it would be a huge success because the gift giver gives this gift from his inner soul with a prayer from the beyond.

The world's most renowned surgeon, my brother Jacobus, only two years older than us, had done his magic through science. Yet I know my brother suffered emotionally internally as he gave a second chance to one brother and we both lost another. The three of us were raised by his biological parents, my uncle and aunt whom I had always called my Big Papa and Big Mama. Big Papa is known as the wisest man on Earth as he does not say much but his silence talks more than any words said aloud.

We never felt like orphans as Big Papa and Big Mama raised us like their own children yet always told us we had a wonderful father and a very kind and loving mother. Life had given my parents a short period of time to celebrate on Earth. Big Papa said Andries and I are the biological sons of his first cousin Petrus van Phillip and his beloved wife, my biological mother, Giada Berlusconi van Phillip. Big Papa grew up in the same house with my father and their cousin Matthias van Phillip.

Uncle Matthias had moved to New Delhi, India and lives with Big Mama's greater family members. He is trying to figure out life's greater purpose and the theory behind reincarnation and dreams. He believes he was reincarnated over and over again for someone or something and wants to find out what it is.

My parents had a short-lived life together with one another. Big Mama had said it is better to be together with your twin flame either in life or in death. My family members celebrate life as a gift and compare it to only one complete day.

There is no regret as we live with the memories of a day to the last breath of our lives. For companions, we all keep our diaries throughout time. Today I too shall bury the pain and loss of my brother and celebrate the memories and live life through his loving eyes, until we meet again.

Tonight I had a strange dream. I was watching my brother Jacobus perform a surgery. The patient was a person he had saved years ago. I watched a child standing at the corner of the room with his tiny hands in a prayer gesture. I heard the sound of heartbeats, yet it was playing on a piano.

I heard Jacobus say, "Come on Katelijne Snaaijer, don't give up on me now. You must fight for your life."

I heard the young child, a baby boy about two years of age, say, "Come on woman, don't give up! I want to go home! She is crying and waiting for me!"

I watched Jacobus talk with his team and say, "Someone had mercilessly raped this young woman and had her tied up for days. We need to know why. This is a police case and I need to find out who committed this outrageous crime. I will keep her alive and get her back on her feet. Everyone will see how a dead person too can come back. Come on woman, don't give up."

I saw the baby boy who looked like Andries and myself. He had thick brown hair. Even his eyes were the perfect shade of my brother's.

He laughed and said, "That's what I said, don't give up. You and I think alike. I like you."

Jacobus inspected the young woman's body and said, "My inner gut feeling is the criminal or criminals were known to her. She trusted them and that's why all the bruises were occurring over time."

I watched my brother go outside and as to his character, he went silent. He always kept his personal feelings buried within himself. Then I followed some nurses as I was now standing in a room that looked too cold. I wondered where I was.

Was this a morgue or what was this place? The whole room felt cold. I saw there were so many people who looked as if they were all just sleeping. Maybe they were all given a sleeping pill and all of them just went to sleep.

All were young women who had a full life left ahead of them, yet their life just stopped like the wall clock which needed new batteries. No one moved, nor did anyone snore. I wondered why there was no sound of heartbeats.

I passed a bed which had the so-called woman whom my brother was trying to save. I don't know if she had died or was just sleeping like all the women in the cold room. I suddenly felt a hand rise from beneath the bedsheets and touch me. Here in front of my blessed eyes was the picturesque portrait of the most beautiful woman. In front of me was a talking portrait of the most beautiful face, a blind man was fortunate to see.

She said, "Please help me. I want justice and I don't want to leave my twin flame and die in vain. Please help and find me, for I await your arrival, my only and last hope."

Then I heard heartbeats and followed the sound and saw the child again as he said, "I am scared. Why am I here? I want to go home now! Take me home, she is crying for me. It's your fault if she gets upset. If you are late, she will be in pain and will hurt more. I don't want her to hurt more. Please take me home now!"

I had awakened to the blue misty and smoky morning of the Great Smoky Mountains. I almost had the urge to call my brother Jacobus or Big Mama and talk to them about my nightmare. I knew my family members all believe in dreams. Yet I didn't want my family to panic over me, so I remained quiet at least until the time comes when I must share my dreams.

Today I would be meeting up with a friend who had traveled to the USA from the Netherlands. He was on a vacation tour around the country. I knew he was going back in a day or two, so before I brought him back to my cabin, we were going to meet up for coffee in town.

I walked past a boutique style bookstore, an internet café which had a huge crowd. I try to avoid huge and crowded cafés. Yet I heard my art college buddy Josquin de Cloet call on me.

He said, "Antonius, listen, could you come over here? I really want to take a free read and want you to get one too. The world's best tarot card reader is giving a free read with our breakfast coffee. She is also the owner of this bookstore. Everyone in our vacationing group has had a good read. I think you really should come over. They have your mother's books for sale here too."

I don't know if it's in my genetics or what, but I could never say no to anyone, unless it was urgent and I could not keep my promises. I also have all of Big Mama's books but if I see her books in any unknown store, I just grab another copy. I guess it just feels strangely good to hold on to another copy of my mother's books.

I watched my best friend who had been there for my brother and had never left my side for the long, lonely nights, as I was separated from my twin by a breath. My family had lost a son that day and from the unknown had gained one in Josquin. He looked so much like us as he had brown hair up to his shoulders and brown eyes. He was six feet, two inches tall just like my brother and myself. He loved Big Mama and collected all of her books.

I had gone over and to my surprise I had enjoyed the company. We had all enjoyed a quiet breakfast, but I had to leave to attend an art gallery news conference nearby. All the big art galleries worldwide were investigating huge murder crimes that were going on around the globe, yet somehow were linked to Dam Square in Amsterdam, the Netherlands.

Somehow the crimes became a huge world news headline as there were no leads. However, all the young girls were worried and were asked to travel in groups. My Big Papa had asked me to attend the meeting and find out if the crimes were limited to Amsterdam only or worldwide. I knew the police also wanted Big Mama's help. As a psychic, she can usually sense trouble or pain if it was around. I promised my group I would return after the news conference.

Driving was a dream I thought would never come and see the daylight. For this dream had a price written on it I could never afford nor did I ever wish for it. As this wish also felt like a curse, I keep on reminding myself not to ever wish for something or curse someone, for what if it comes true?

I returned to a small village looking area, after my much-needed time alone and the meetings I had to go on yet could have avoided. No one knew what was going on with the murders for they seemed worldwide yet somehow all linked back to Amsterdam and some paintings or portraits of the murdered victims. I thought I wouldn't mention any of this to the vacationers as I didn't want to rain on their parade.

I was glad I was late for I must have missed the tarot card reader in the meanwhile. I so eagerly prayed and wished I had missed it. As I reached a small café near Dollywood, I knew I would again have the blessing to see my friend whom I had seen for the first time with sight after my surgery. I had a lot of catching up to do which was not possible in one coffee meeting.

I still walk with my white cane as it was my support and a gift from my Big Mama. I had promised my mother I would never forget it. Even with my sight, I still keep my promise.

I heard someone had uttered my name, so my sixth sense had turned toward the sound. Even though life had taken away my sight, I was gifted with my sixth sense from birth. Today even with sight, I still am alerted by my sixth sense.

A woman in a crowd of people had said, "You are the blind painter Antonius van Phillip! The famous painter who paints everything in black and white. You are the nephew of the famous Dutch painter Erasmus van Phillip and the famous author, the dream psychic, Anadhi Newhouse van Phillip. I have just purchased some of your mother's famous books."

I watched her for a while as if I knew her yet I could not place a name or place to her. I wondered if I had known her from before my sight. Yet she cleared out the air in between us, as if she could read my mind.

She said, "No we have never met, but I have been expecting you. I know you too hear the heartbeats that have been playing like a piano around you."

I wondered what she meant by that, yet it's true I had been hearing the sound of heartbeats around me. It's also true they never sound scary or boring but like a pianist playing on his piano. I should know as my twin brother was a famous pianist and a composer. Even to this day, his musical compositions remain chartbusters.

I was deep in my world of thoughts when my friend Josquin came out from the small cabin. He approached me and gave me a bear hug. A habit he picked up during his travels, one of his favorite acts yet not a very Dutch-like characteristic. Touring through the USA and working for my uncle's company had earned him some very nice American touches.

After my brother's death, Josquin had taken over my brother's work burden for my uncle. He loved this gift of hugs and gestures of just pure kindness. For in the Netherlands, we don't show much of our emotions. That's why I guess the outside world says the Dutch reputation is we are cold, direct, talk bluntly, and kiss on our cheeks but are not big huggers.

My friend said, "This is Marinda, a psychic, also the famous tarot card reader. She is of Dutch ancestry and knows Kasteel Vrederic very well. She is actually a descendant of the van Vrederic family psychic, Aunt Marinda. She wanted to meet you as she said she has some urgent messages for you, from the beyond as you too are one of the direct descendants of the van Vrederic family."

The psychic we were talking about watched both of us as she said bluntly without even wasting a minute, "One of you will have a very good summer if you so will. Yet the other one of you must return home to the Netherlands for your dead twin flame awaits your arrival. It won't be hard as all you must do is follow the musical heartbeats of the little one."

We watched her and thought she must have misspoken or something. For I wondered how a dead person could wait for a living person at all. Yet I knew she was not a normal person as she was somehow related to my forefathers. I only wondered what else life had in store for me.

She said, "You must fall in love with a dead woman. For after you fall in love with her, it is then you are the only one who can keep her alive or give her life. This could be through your pull for your twin flame and your family members' miraculous gifts, devotion, persistence, and belief that a bond never ends as long as the heartbeats keep pulling one toward the other. Remember following your interlinking dreams, she will find you as you will find her. Your family members will guide you from behind you always. I believe you are the brother of my Jacobus van Vrederic incarnate. I will always follow Jacobus and his family members throughout eternity as promised from beyond."

Marinda then stopped as she was looking at Big Mama's book and smiled to herself. She then said, "This is your destiny. Do not fear your destiny as you too are a son of this blessed family. Remember if you try to avoid this destiny in fear then you will not know what love is. For it is sometimes getting acquainted with death that teaches you the meaning of life and true love. Ahh well yes, I do know your family members are very well acquainted with death. It's a pain they have buried within themselves as they have buried so many. Yet they live with the hope of reincarnation and dreams, so must you."

She stopped talking as if she was gathering her thoughts. Marinda was a very famous psychic in her own field, yet if I am correct, then she is a time traveler and only appears when the family members of Kasteel Vrederic need her.

Marinda then said, "Your Big Mama and I had become acquainted with one another during a devastating bus accident that had taken away her dear family members. Yet faith and dreams of her twin flame had kept her hope alive. Please tell her to not give up on him, as he too is ripping the world and heavens apart to be back with her. Ahh yes, all of you follow the heartbeats. Yes, also give my Jacobus a message for me and tell him I will see him back in the seventeenth century soon."

I was correct and she is the same psychic my parents had spoken about. I knew what she was talking about as I had read Big Mama and Big Papa's diary, *Be My Destiny: Vows From The Beyond*, quite a few times. I love my parents so much for their devotion toward one another and toward their faith in true love. Yet we all knew this famous psychic had promised the famous diarist Jacobus van Vrederic she would always throughout eternity keep an eye on the family members of Kasteel Vrederic. She too knew the famous diarist had come back as Jacobus Vrederic van Phillip.

She then just walked away as if she wouldn't talk anymore. I wondered would she be able to travel back in time to the seventeenth century? For she looked so much like the late sixteenth-century psychic, Aunt Marinda of Kasteel Vrederic, whose portrait made by sixteenth-century Jacobus van Vrederic still hangs to this day within our ancestral home. I knew she was the same person, for even today her love for Jacobus is the same, like a mother or an aunt who never lets him or his memories fade away.

Then I heard Josquin say, "So I was supposed to be traveling back to the Netherlands tomorrow. You were going to spend your summer in Tennessee. Yet I believe you should travel back home and I will stay at your home. That way, we can both complete our vacation in peace. By switching places, we also switch our fate and nothing will happen to either one of us. Yet I am confused was she talking about me or you? She is your family psychic, so I am confident she was talking about you."

I watched my friend as I knew he was shaking in fear of falling in love with a dead woman. I knew he believed in psychic readers like a mantra and would never doubt them. I usually doubted unless they were related to Kasteel

Vrederic. I knew if my family members were at risk or were involved in this in any kind or form, I would be on the next plane to Amsterdam Airport Schiphol and no one on this planet could stop me.

I told him, "I will be on the next flight to Amsterdam."

In my mind, I thought how I could miss Big Mama so much. I missed her smell and her Indian cooking more than I thought was possible. I also missed her sitting next to my bed until I fall asleep. I actually wouldn't get upset anymore when she rubs my hair with argan oil. I had left the Netherlands yet I felt like I left my mind, body, and soul within the kind and loving tears of my Big Mama.

From a very young age of barely a few months old, I had known her as my Big Mama, not Aunt Anadhi. She had with all her love raised me, my twin, and her only son, Jacobus, like her own three sons. I was going home to my Big Mama. As when and where I feel lost or stranded, it is then my Big Papa and Big Mama had always held on to my hands.

Unfortunately, I have no memories of my biological parents. My parents were always my Big Papa and Big Mama. Yet Big Papa had taken us aside when we were seven years old and told us about the horrific car accident that had taken our parents away from us. A drunk driver had mercilessly caused the accident where he too was a prey of his own doing.

My father was Big Papa's first cousin as their mothers were triplets, whom I never got to see. They had passed away peacefully on the same day, together during one of their travels through India. They were born together and they had passed away together too. It was hard for the family yet I know that's what they had wished and their prayers were answered.

I kept on hearing Big Mama and her words, "Mama's heart beats my three big boys."

I told her mind to mind, "I am coming home Big Mama."

That night on the flight to Amsterdam, I had another dream. I watched a dead woman walking in an art studio all dressed in white. She was stuck in a mirror and kept on asking me to hurry as she was having a hard time breathing.

I also saw in front of the mirror, there was a child, a baby boy. He kept banging on the mirror and said, "Woman, get up and take me home. Had I not told you she is crying, and I miss her? You know I did not even take her permission to go. I must go back home."

The mystical princess only said, "My love, did you meet Aunt Marinda? Was she able to give you the message for I await your arrival? I am Katelijne. Please don't forget the fortune teller's warning."

Dear beloved, I won't forget you or any warnings for here is my second poem I have written only for you.

FORTUNE TELLER'S WARNING

From within my inner soul, I seek you.
Yet I only find you in my sweet dreams.
Wishing to sleep by your side
At all times, only to see
I sleep alone and awaken all alone.
Your sweet, hot tears warm my chest
During my dreams.

Yet I find out my pillows are covered

With my hot tears of the night.

Craving for a miracle to take place

In the dark night's sweet dreams,

Yet I find only the visions

Of my leftover sweet memories of you.

I know you are hiding within a mirror

Yet at all times watching over me.

May my love be there with you,

Watching over you throughout eternity.

Be safe, be mine,

For how could I hear my heart beat,

If your heart beats no more?

I will find you in heavens above,

Or Earth beneath,

For I will not overlook or disrespect the,

FORTUNE TELLER'S WARNING.

Signed: Antonius van Phillip

CHAPTER TWO:

Escaping Destiny

"Call upon your destiny. Go and greet her. Walk to her and let your footsteps create the path. Never fear the path for the path is of your making. Let life be made out through your dreams, and do not fear or worry about escaping destiny."

As Antonius van Phillip stands in front of the Lover's Lighthouse and as his feet accidently touch the box holding his beloved's portrait, the spirits of Kasteel Vrederic appear to bless him.

T he Netherlands is my destiny which I have chosen even when I had the choice to choose or not. Within each birth, I shall only choose you if I could, or if you too wish for me to be your child, dear land. For within this land, my Big Mama found her destiny.

She chose to be here with her twin flame and make a home for themselves and all of their children. The Netherlands is a small Western European country, where the canals and the tulip fields are musical notes for the artist drawing her on his or her canvas. The windmills spread the smell of fresh baked bread and cheese around the land, as she greets all her permanent and temporary visitors.

I have a small apartment in Amsterdam, the nation's capital, even though Den Haag is the famous political capital. Today though I would go directly to Kasteel Vrederic, my family home in Naarden, a city about twenty minutes away from Amsterdam Airport Schiphol. For within this home, lives the only woman I have lost my heart to. She always told her three sons, "Mama's heart beats my three boys."

As she raised me, she had covered her own eyes and walked in the dark to grasp the world from the sight of her blind son. She learned to walk with a cane as she taught me and herself to live with this disability for her son. She told me she was not my birth mother as my parents had passed away when I was too young to understand. Yet she became my mother and has proven to this world, you don't need to give birth to be a mother for her heart beats for all three of us.

After my twin brother passed away, she became my support and taught me again how to live with sight. A mother had lost her son. Yet because of her love for her twin son, she buried her pain as she buried one twin and became the strength for the other twin. During the night when she assumes all of her children are sleeping, she cries like the night's singing birds. She walks to his gravesite not far from our home and sings to him. I had followed her some nights and could not bear her pain, yet she never lets us see her pain.

So we too let her handle it her way. Big Papa follows her in the dark and he too keeps quiet and lets her deal with it her own way. Yet he never leaves his twin flame alone as like all of us, he too wants her to be safe.

She sings every night by his gravesite, "My beloved son, you are sleeping so calmly, yet how does this mother of yours sleep tonight, for being separated from you keeps me awake throughout the nights. Yet I shall be brave during the days for your brothers and Papa. My baby boy, come back to Mama for this Mama shall call you throughout eternity. My baby boy, how does a mother sleep peacefully in bed when her son is getting drenched with cold pouring rain showers? I know my brave young man, you are older now and don't fear the thunderstorms, yet I still hear you crawling into my bed as you used to say you were not afraid but wanted to keep your Big Mama safe from the thunderstorms. I am scared now. I need you to hold on to me, come back to me now, and hold my hands my baby boy please."

The sun was setting in the amazing night skies as I reached home. I realized the night too knew a son has returned home to his mother, as the skies made an amazing twinkling show out of the stars appearing all around. If I could pick up the feelings and wrap them up like a gust of wind, then this world would know a mother awaits her son.

A father was trying to keep his wife calm as she must have caused flowers to grow all around through her worries for me. I saw forget-me-nots were blooming with love all around our home. I knew they were my mother's love and teardrops that blossomed all around our home.

My very small, petite mother was waiting out in the courtyard of our home. The legendary Lover's Lighthouse was shining on top of our home, Kasteel Vrederic. Rumor is, when twin flames pray in front of the lighthouse and if their prayers get answered, one will see the eternal twin flames Griet and Theunis in the lighthouse. I had always wondered before my sight how would my prayers be answered as one must see the spirits of Kasteel Vrederic.

My twin brother Andries had said, "Since we are twins and I do have the sight yet you have the looks, I will guide your twin flame to you, as my heart beats my brother's name, after Big Mama and Big Papa's names."

He was always joking about looks yet we were twins and everyone had said it was like looking at the mirror. I had wanted to see him at least once. Now I do as I look into the mirror and see the past in the mirror of my memories.

I told him mind to mind, "Andries go and find her for me, will you? She is in danger so bring her home to me. Hey bro, also please somehow come back home, if you can as Big Mama can't take it anymore. She believes you are coming back home. Even though we told her you are at a place from where you can't come back home. I believe in Big Mama and she is waiting for you, so please try."

Everyone would keep on saying to pray in front of the lighthouse. So I had asked my big brother Jacobus, how could I pray in front of the lighthouse when I can't even see the twin flames?

He had said, "It is you who can't see them. Whoever said they can't see you? If my intuitive feeling about the two lovebirds in the lighthouse is right, then I believe they will come to you."

I never asked him as to how he knew, as I knew he was the incarnation of the legendary diarist Jacobus van Vrederic. He was born with complete memories of his past life while others in the family acquired the memories through sudden shock or accidents that had jerked the memories back to them. Yet Jacobus knew all the events surrounding the time period of the famous diarist.

I was staring at the amazing lighthouse on top of our home glowing ever so brightly when a sudden sound of a very common soft voice jerked all of my inner feelings for a mother, dispensing out tears from my eyes. I never showed my feelings through tears in front of anyone but in front of this woman, they just flowed without fear.

Big Mama said, "My son is back home. Tonight I can sleep in peace as at least I have one of you I can hold within my chest. Even though I had thought I should have kept all three of you in my inner chest always. One of my sons sleeps in his deep sleep under the blue skies and took all of Mama and Papa's sleep with him."

I could not speak as words never came to me easily, for I had my twin brother do the talking while I just listened to my words being played in front of me, even without saying anything. I watched my father, Big Papa, just watch me. He could say everything in this world without uttering anything. I knew as he had walked into the room without even saying anything, he would get his ways.

Big Papa just watched me and gave a son and his mother some space. My very handsome father and beautiful mother looked more like a young couple rather than parents as they were both born with evergreen looks. A son today watched his parents who had remembered their vows from the beyond even when rebirth and obstacles of life had tested them.

Big Papa said, "So, my son, I hear you have not created any new paintings in three years? I believe your vacation has ended and now we go back into training to teach you to paint with sight."

I knew Big Papa knew everything without saying anything. It was Big Papa who had taught his blind son to paint without any sight. He had placed a blindfold on himself as he placed a blank canvas and brush in my hands. Seeing the world through a blindfold, he knew exactly how I could not see anything, yet he never let this be an obstacle.

So over the years, it was this amazing teacher who had taught his son, the blind student, to become the famous blind painter. Everything I had painted in black and white. Today I watched the famous painter Erasmus van Phillip and knew admiration and devotion could not explain my eternal love and honor I have for my Big Papa.

Big Papa said, "My son, life is a blessing as with each departure, we have an arrival. Your brother Jacobus just left for Africa where he will perform some of his miracle surgeries. Your Mama and Papa need one of our sons to be awake and with us as your other brother had decided to go to sleep and won't wake up even after so many calls. Maybe with you home, I can get your Big Mama to sleep tonight."

I knew Big Mama says her son Andries was asleep in the garden of *Evermore Beloved*. She would never say he was gone but only asleep until it was his time to return again. It was her way of moving on with grace and honor. A mother who mourned her son even more than anyone would say or utter in this house, yet she kept on telling this world she would pull him back to her chest, it's only a matter of time.

Big Papa said, "Tomorrow you will start your lessons, as this is a new journey for you. I know you learned to paint in the dark, but now the light is on and the painter too must adjust to his newfound environment."

I watched the lighthouse was blinking suddenly, as Big Mama screamed and said, "Watch the lighthouse glow! And there in the lighthouse is a kissing couple!"

Big Mama held on to Big Papa as she said, "This is the first time in years they have returned. I wonder why or how, as there are no new twin flames in search of one another facing the Lover's Lighthouse. Erasmus, do you think it's a sign, Andries is coming back?"

I observed my parents watch the lighthouse that never has been wrong in centuries. My foot touched something in the dark night as there were boxes stored on the porch for some reason, very unlike my very organized parents. Upon close inspection, it seemed all of the boxes had yellow tape on them.

Yet one box laid open under the glowing lights of the Lover's Lighthouse. There in front of us was a painting. An artist had captured a beautiful young woman's pain and tears so vividly on the portrait. I thought the woman looked so familiar yet I could not place my mind to it. Where had I seen her? It had to be in the last three years after my vision, but where?

Big Mama said, "Erasmus, the paintings from the crime scene have opened somehow. Why were they left here? And by whom?"

I asked my parents, "What crime scene are you two talking about? What happened here? Does Jacobus know what is going on here? Why on Earth are you two left here alone with things from a crime scene?"

I was so scared for my parents I wanted to shout out and tell them I am still alive, so why were they dealing with these things on their own? Yet I only had whispers frozen within my lips as I could never get angry or even say anything to the two people standing in front of me. I felt like my heartbeat would freeze if I even tried to be mad at them. With God as my witness, how could I love them so much? It's their innocent blank stares. They were trying to fool me.

My Big Mama watched me and ran toward me as she said, "What were you thinking? I don't know, but remember my heart beats all three of my sons. I don't really care where you three are, above or beyond this Earth. My heart beats all three of your names. Just watch how I shall never let any one of you go. I will bring all of you back to my heart. Hear this, my heart beats for my three sons, and the love of my life, your Big Papa. I never let him go, not in one lifetime or others as true love never fades even beyond time."

Big Papa came and picked up the painting as he said, "I was given these portrait paintings by the police. They are of murder victims. A ruthless killer had captured young women as he, or she, or they then painted these portraits as the girls were being tortured. The paintings brought a lot of money through tasteless, cheap people who love to see tragedy, pain, and sufferings, and paid a lot for them."

Big Papa watched the glowing lighthouse and said, "I had asked you to attend the conference at the art gallery in Tennessee for the same reason. I was in touch with the crime branch to see if I could help solve this cold case. The paintings started to arrive to art dealers about three years ago. While the paintings were of missing girls, somehow, the girls, living or dead, were eventually found. Their faces resembled their last fear as if their attacker's fingerprints were imprinted on their portraits which can only be seen through the eyes of a painter. So I will try to see if I can tell anything about the artist who did the paintings. Maybe that way, we can bring in some closure for the families of the victims."

I watched my Big Mama as she said, "Jacobus knows one of the girls as he had tried to save her once. I don't know who hurt her and why, but she had some heart problems Jacobus was treating her for. She lived with her stepfather as her mother died when she was young. Her stepfather is devastated according to Jacobus."

Big Mama kept on looking at the lighthouse. She said, "They have a small cottage in Amsterdam, and she also worked for a hotel where most of these portraits were found. Yet the owners don't have a clue of what happened to all the girls and where all the portraits came from or how the women had gone missing from their hotel without them having any clues. They though said they fired her after she never came back to work. How do you fire a missing dead person? I have no clue."

I watched Big Papa take the painting in his hands as he said, "She passed away three years ago, and your brother still believes she is alive and has her on life support. Yet the hospital declared her dead. I don't know if she was buried or kept somewhere secretly as Jacobus won't say anything, and we won't pry. I am paying for her care myself as your brother never said if she is really on life support or dead. I guess it's a police case and your brother was her physician."

I never asked my parents why did they want her to be alive? Why were they paying for her expenses? If she was alive or if she had died, I did not ask.

I saw the painting and I told Big Mama, "I saw her in my dream. She asked me to help her. I watched her and other women in a morgue or some kind of place. By the way, I also saw Jacobus trying to save them. I then saw her cold hands had touched me and she asked me to help her."

Big Papa then said, "I know Josquin called us and spoke to us or confessed about him avoiding to be the guinea pig. So he switched places with you. I also heard you had seen Aunt Marinda, or her lookalike, who had prophesied one of you would fall in love with a dead person. I don't know what to say but I would not actually avoid Aunt Marinda's warnings. She had also warned your Big Mama before a sudden tragedy did hit her, yet it was then we also found one another."

He touched Big Mama and held on to her tightly within his chest. Big Papa's love for Big Mama and her love for him awakened our faith in twin flames. Big Papa watched me for a while.

He then said, "Life is a journey. We will cross the path as we are confronted with destiny, yet your Mama and I believe in creating our own destiny. We call upon destiny and never are afraid of it. I know my son, you too would not avoid destiny but call upon it and confront it your way."

I watched Big Papa and started to laugh as I said, "Big Papa, we all know my friend Josquin is not the person who would be anywhere near dead people. Remember why he had left medical college in his second year? It was a dead body. He ran from the psychic when he heard the words. Yet here I don't know why I am pulled toward that face, the painting that came from nowhere and landed upon my feet. Also it is strange at the same time, the kissing couple appeared in the Lover's Lighthouse."

Big Mama watched the Lover's Lighthouse and said, "Dear Griet and Theunis, you are my Jacobus's daughter and son-in-law, and my Rietje's parents. So why can't you a parent help and guide my son Andries back home to me? Don't worry, I will call him back home to me as you will all see how he comes back home to me."

I could not stop my tears from falling for a woman I love more than my own existence, so I too asked Andries, in my mind, to come back somehow.

Big Papa was the only one watching the Lover's Lighthouse as he said, "There is a child in the lighthouse and there is a sound coming from it. A piano is playing a heartbeat."

Big Mama cried and said, "Yes, my baby boy I know, Mama's heart beats all three of my boys."

I wondered who were they? The child now even my parents could see, and her, the mystical princess. Why did the spirits appear in the Lover's Lighthouse as her portrait came and landed upon my feet? Why was the child linked with her or were they two separate issues? I watched the portrait and thought whoever you are, you don't belong near anyone's feet but within someone's chest.

I gazed at the dark star-filled night watching my family spirits in the lighthouse and said, "The sitter of the portrait, whoever you are, wherever you are, I will find justice for you. I know a dead person can't be my destiny but in this family, we believe in creating our own destiny even beyond the grave. So if we are to be together, then let it be. Let us be destined to destiny and let these be my vows from the beyond."

Then I only prayed in my mind, "Dear stranger, I promise you will escape death, for this story is not about the living or dead. In this home, we only believe in eternity. For love is eternal and in love, my Big Mama always says you are destined to your created destiny. So to accept the destiny you want, you must then let go of the one given to you. Destined to destiny is what we choose. So we learn and teach all life is not destined to destiny for we the living and the dead are separated by a breath, but it's because some of us survive by escaping destiny."

My beloved, I have not forgotten you or
my given oath. I have written a poem for
you tonight too, as even though the
nights are long and the days are even
longer, this is my sweet gift for
my beloved from her beloved.
Poem number three.

ESCAPING DESTINY

Lover's Lighthouse guides all true lovers
To one another.
Tonight this magical lighthouse

Has called upon us too,
Yet I ask you my love, can you hear me?
Do you feel me through
Our passionate night's sweet dreams?
Are my thoughts your blessings
Throughout the days
While you are away from me?
My love, your sweet calls of the nights
Are my endurance scarf
Throughout the lonely days.
My heart's dear beholder,
Why don't you come now and

Reclaim me as your heart's beholder?

For fear not the heavens,

Fear not the Earth,

Fear not destiny,

But live life within the embrace

Of your beloved by,

ESCAPING DESTINY.

Signed: Antonius van Phillip

CHAPTER THREE:

A Gift For The Host

"Guests are blessings in disguise, however, at times one only wonders would one invite a guest who will unbury the secrets you would rather leave buried? Or were you the host seeking answers and so forth opened your doors to the guests whose presence becomes a gift for the host?"

*Antonius van Phillip saw in his dream, Katelijne
Snaaijer was being attacked by dark shadows.*

T he night skies were singing romantic musical notes as I watched the nightly concert in my family courtyard. I had spent my entire life basically here yet in the dark. I had always allowed my imagination of the night to create a picture in my mind and had created all my paintings, my art, through this blessed door. My brother was my sight as he always stood by me describing everything he saw in detail. My artistic skills were one of my family's biggest gifts given to me.

Forever the world was what I saw through my family. I saw love through Big Mama's eyes. I became strong and brave as I was held with bravery and strength within the embrace of my Big Papa. I learned to be independent and kept my emotions hidden within my inner self as I learned this skill from my brother Jacobus, the diarist incarnate.

My biggest inspiration in life is my big brother. If I had ever fallen or gotten hurt, I would search in the dark for my big brother. His comforting words had always guided me out of the darkness I lived within.

All he had to say was, "Everything will be just all right."

My big brother's favorite phrase that still holds the power to it. I wanted to ask him again yet I repeated this phrase to myself. I told myself, I will make everything just all right for my family, for my Big Mama, my Big Papa, and my honorable big brother.

So tonight in front of the Lover's Lighthouse, I took a vow of an honorable man. I will avenge the painful death portrayed by a painter who hides in the dark for I am a man who had lived in the dark as it was my Creator's will. We are both artists yet you chose the dark path where nothing is born but everything ends. I have chosen the path that glows with promises from the Lover's Lighthouse of ever after, here hope glows from heart to heart.

I will catch you through the learned techniques of my blindness that was my life-long partner. Yet tonight I am in the light as I have the blessed gift of sight, and I will bring back light to all of these unjustly, brutally murdered victims of the dark evil monster, who looms around hiding in the dark.

I watched Big Mama and Big Papa dance in the courtyard as they are in my eyes, the most loving couple on this Earth. Twin flames that have loved one another throughout time. Here I have witnessed them to love all of their children, family, and friends unconditionally. I knew Big Papa wanted to solve this mystery and somehow my psychic Big Mama knew more than she was sharing. Yet I wouldn't ask her as she would never share her dreams without proof of the day.

I stood in front of the two people I love the most on this Earth and said, "People can lie and make up their stories. They can hide the truth, yet science does not. For science always follows the truth which shall always leave a trail to the predator through his or her crimes committed. I shall follow the truth with the blessed gifts of my two brothers, one a doctor and a scientist, and the other who has blessed me with my sight. For I believe I will be able to solve this cold case that still haunts all young women at night."

My parents watched me as they never interrupted me while I was trying to organize my thoughts. I wondered if they were born with patience. Or maybe we the three brothers had made them become patient.

I continued, "No woman shall ever suffer like this, as I can feel and touch the pain of these women the police call subjects. These portraits show not just subjects or sitters of a portrait, but premeditated insights of a beast who made pain and suffering his or her joy."

Big Papa asked, "How do you plan to do that? I know you want to solve this yet it might be dangerous as we don't know if we are dealing with one person or a group. This person or group has killed a lot of young women across the globe. Yet the person always made a portrait of the murder victims."

Big Papa took a break as he was playing with Big Mama's hair. I knew this from childhood. He would just watch her for hours or minutes and make a portrait of her. Again he at times just watched her and I thought it felt like he could watch her all of his life and still not get tired of it. This is love, when you just want to watch one another at times for hours or maybe at times just a peek. Inspiration for my inner soul as I am the inspired.

Then Big Papa asked me, "I realized you have done a lot of research on these murder victims. The common theory is easy. A portrait was created at the murder scene. Yet why?"

I told Big Papa, "I don't believe there was a portrait created at the time of the murder. I believe the murderer took a picture of the murder victim and the murder scene. It very well could have been a live video. He or she then recreated the picture through a computer that was programmed to recreate a picture to look like a hand-drawn portrait. Also at times, it seemed they messed up as some of them look like pencil sketches which were again done on a computer to look like hand-painted sketches. A lot of fake artworks have been found using these techniques. If honestly told that they were recreated from a picture through a computer programmed to look like a hand-drawn portrait, it would be all right. Because both creators are artists, one does it through his or her hands, while the other does it through technology."

I watched Big Papa smile and watch me as I knew of course he knew for he was my teacher. I knew he had figured out these were recreated through a program that is rare yet an artist with eyes can catch it. Yet why were they being sold saying they were hand-created paintings and sketches?

I told him, "I will pretend to be blind as that's how I can catch the culprit at his or her own game. I will go and stay at the same hotel the victims' portraits were discovered within. My dreams have led me to this hotel in Amsterdam where I keep on seeing a woman stand in the window, or in a mirror crying for me to be quick as she does not have much time. At all times standing with her or next to her is a child, a baby boy, crying and asking to be quick."

I watched Big Mama and told her, "Big Mama, you have given this gift to me your adopted son. For I believe no blood could be stronger than your love for me and my love for you, as this is why my heart always beats your name. For the same reason, I too am a dream psychic. I see the future and the past in the dark nights as my dreams have helped me travel through places others can't go to. Yet I keep on hearing heartbeats whenever I see the woman and the child. The heartbeats sound like a piano playing in the background."

Big Mama was watching me like a worried mother as I saw her tears betray her and she spilled them without even trying to hide them. I knew she knew much more than she did share but neither I nor Big Papa said anything.

She then surprised everyone as she said, "Erasmus and I will help you. Your Big Papa and you have an apartment above the family art studio there. We can move into your apartment in Amsterdam and we will be there with you."

I kissed my mother and said, "Big Mama, anytime you want, we can go over there, yet today we need to check in to the infamous hotel where all the paintings were found."

Big Mama then said, "Okay, so we check in to the hotel, a family suite. We can all pretend to be there to maybe help you or we will see how the wave goes and deal with it. I will be by my son to help with the investigation."

She then started to face the ground as she said, "I already called a few vacation rentals and I have asked some antiques dealers and art dealers about who are buying these artworks. It must be some kind of dark business. Some of these people run dirty businesses from their homes."

She was talking nonstop as she does when she is nervous, "The strangest part was I checked out the hotel owners. They are originally from Eindhoven, Noord-Brabant. They have a daughter who is about forty years old and never was married, never known to have dated, and never goes out. She travels all the time managing her parents' boutique hotels around the globe. I wonder with all of the hotels around the nation and internationally, why would they still run a small boutique hotel on their own? Their international chains are handled with hired employees. Here they only had the one woman."

I was shocked at Big Mama's intervention, yet I knew as did Big Papa, the dream psychic, my Big Mama, knew much more than she would share. Big Mama knew where the story begins and at times where or how it might end. It's then she gets involved to change the outcome as some are warnings of what to avoid.

I wanted to ask my Big Mama so much more about the woman who comes and visits me at night. When all is dark and nothing can be heard, I hear her and I can even smell her, but how do I see and feel a woman I never knew in my life? Why do I hear her heartbeats nonstop? I never got to utter the words as I saw my two favorite grandmothers run out of the door like a whirlwind.

One was Big Mama's maternal grandmother who is of Indian ancestry. We all call her Nani. The other one was Big Mama's paternal grandmother, an American yet mixed with Dutch ancestry. We all call her Grandmother.

They both were brought over to Kasteel Vrederic as Big Mama does not believe elders should be stored away in a home far away when they are in their golden years. She wants to have more time with everyone rather than regretting time lost due to distance and life's gift of limited days. Big Papa says as long as he has his twin flame, he too loves family as he misses his mother and aunts.

I never knew these women were Jacobus's bloodline, not mine, as they taught me family is those of whom we choose to have in this home. The two women became best friends over the years. Nani is short and chubby and very lovingly cute. Grandmother is tall and slender and a very stern woman yet once you get to know her, she is the most loving person on this Earth aside from Nani. Both have gray hair and are very energetic and elegant for their age. They raised the three of us alongside Big Mama and Big Papa.

Nani said, "My boys are here, are all three of you here? I have been waiting for all three of you. I can't even die in peace without you three by my side. So I told the

Angel of Death to stay away until I can hold on to the three of you."

My Dutch-American great-grandmother then said, "My child, where are your two brothers, Andries and Jacobus? It's not fair you all come at different times. We miss them too. I can't believe your sight has been restored by Jacobus. Yet I know you three need to settle down and be together."

Big Papa wiped his eyes as he nodded and told me mind to mind not to say anything. From the corner, I saw Big Mama hide her emotions and say, "The boys will all come home. I promise you two will finally get to scream at them when they do finally come. I just want to hug them first, and then I will let you two have them."

I went and hugged my two favorite grandmothers and told Nani, "I missed your cooking and can't wait for my dinner. What have you two made tonight? I want to eat first then I catch up with my two girlfriends, on all the time we lost."

I realized my parents still had not told anyone about my brother's death as they believed it might be too much to handle for these beautiful women. I watched Big Papa and Big Mama walk to the lighthouse and pray. I too followed them with my eyes and prayed for a break in the cold case. I so wanted to find out if the dead woman was my twin flame. For then how do we unite? In life or in death? I kept on thinking who was the child as I heard the urgency and fear in his voice.

That night, we all had a very big Indian meal, with fresh baked bread that still comes as a gift from the spirits of Kasteel Vrederic. I watched Big Mama with her signs of sobbing red eyes, sitting very quietly for only a few minutes. For everyone knew Big Mama never hides her emotions as she spills all of it in front of Big Papa. Yet she is not the person who would take away anyone's happiness even at the expense of her own.

Big Mama told me, "Tomorrow we all go to Amsterdam as we will visit your Big Papa's art studio and stay at the boutique hotel. I just wish my other boys were here too. I don't like going to a hotel without my three screaming boys."

I knew this was leading somewhere as then I watched my parents watch one another quietly for a while. I never thought they were actually coming along but I did not say anything as I watched Big Mama and asked in my mind, "Okay Jacobus, where are you?"

Big Papa then said, "You will pay a visit to the famous boutique hotel owners, as they are always looking out for expensive original artworks at a bargain. I have arranged the portrait you so much liked to be gifted to the hotel owners, for I believe they have an eye for strange pictures. They have invited us over to their Amsterdam hotel called the Mirrorless Hotel."

I watched Big Papa for a while and knew what he was saying, as I always said, my father knows best. I told them, "I would love to pay them a visit as they are then our host. How long have we booked the hotel for?"

Big Papa said, "One month. We have it reserved for a month. We told them our apartment is undergoing some renovations and we needed a place for a while since the famous blind painter Antonius van Phillip, my son, will be creating some of his famous artwork there. They are very excited to meet you. And it is my wish you recreate an art sketch of the woman in the portrait, blindly. Tie a scarf on your eyes and recreate it in black and white. You will then take it as a gift for the host."

I wonder how Big Papa knew me so well as he knew I did not want to part with the painting that has haunted me in my dreams. So he asked me to recreate one. Yet I know I will recreate one from my dreams as I saw her during her last hour. I will add the figure that had tortured her in the background like a shadow. I wonder why I thought I always saw a very frightful woman was hunting her or had her hunted down. All of this we would do as I would pretend to be blind.

The night could not have gone by any faster as I kept on painting with memories of my dreams where I saw a beautiful woman was tortured for being beautiful. The first night back in Kasteel Vrederic, I saw another dream. I saw a woman crying and begging she is not beautiful and she never wants to hurt anyone so why was she being tortured. I heard a whisper from behind where a person spoke faking his or her voice through a machine.

The person said, "I will have you raped so no one ever wants to touch you again. I hate you and I believe this way I can stop you from even being desired by anyone else."

As dawn came in front of me, I watched the black and white art I created in the night was watching over me like she too knew she has a second chance and I am her bridge to freedom. So I named the art, *Bridge of Mercy*. This dawn, I spoke loudly in front of the Lover's Lighthouse of Kasteel Vrederic, "Dear Lover's Lighthouse, I will bring her back home somehow. Yet today I have my artwork, which I will take to the hotel, as this is a gift for the host."

My dear beloved, I hope you are still breathing on this Earth. If not, then I promise even with a heavy heart, I won't stop breathing for I will breathe for you. Here is my fourth poem written from my inner soul only for you.

A GIFT FOR THE HOST

My love, my darling,
My mystical princess of the night.
Let my sweet nectar-filled words
Awaken you tonight.
Why not dream a little about us

On this sacred musical night?
Do you not hear my calls,
My beloved beholder
Of my sweet dreams?
Just tonight,
Will you stay awake with me
Until the glorious dawn
Comes upon us?
For my beloved,
With all my affection,
And all my love,
I ask you to keep on believing
In our union and our love story,

For I see you in the nights
Within my dreams
Yet I will find you
In the coming dawns of the future.
For you and only you,
I become a guest,
Where your host gave you only pain,
Even then we shall teach
This world only love.
With all my love,
I shall bring you back
To me with love and tenderness,
As for you,

I too have become a guest,

Of the same dreaded home,

For today I have

Your amazing portrait with me as,

A GIFT FOR THE HOST.

Signed: Antonius van Phillip

CHAPTER FOUR:

Magical Portrait

"Twin flames are mirror images. Even though you can break the mirror or remove the person, you can't separate twin flames for they see one another in the mirror of their eyes. For their portraits of one another become the magical portrait."

*Antonius van Phillip walks into the hotel lobby with his
parents where they are greeted by music composed by
his dead brother Andries van Phillip, and the very
familiar sound of heartbeats.*

The Mirrorless Hotel sits on the banks of the Prinsengracht, one of the four main canals of the Grachtengordel in Amsterdam, the Netherlands. The other three main canals are the Herengracht, the Keizersgracht, and the Singel. During the Dutch Golden Age in the 17th century, all of these canals were created. Along the canals are also about 1,500 monumental buildings that still stand tall retelling the history of the country's capital city.

The Mirrorless Hotel was built in the early 19th century. This hotel is somewhat famous for being one of the most haunted hotels in the capital city. A capital that has a lot of rumors of old ghosts and famous haunting legends that over time have become tourist attractions. Yet this hotel has been rumored to be haunted by made-up ghost stories created solely for the purpose of luring guests to the hotel. Or that's what people think or maybe that's what the owners want people to think. As long as the owners are not doing anything to make it haunted.

Big Mama and Big Papa came with me to spend the day in the famous capital city, even though they live in the greater Amsterdam area and we have our own apartment nearby. I knew my Big Mama wanted to keep an eye out for her son and Big Papa still was not familiar with a blind son driving with his newfound sight. All my life, I had accompanied Big Papa to his art studio which is now one of the most famous art studios in the world.

I learned all my skills in this studio where Andries, the famous pianist, loved to sing and play the piano for Big Mama. He would stay awake and play for her as she would hum with him. It was father and son for me and mother and son for my twin brother. She never touched the piano ever since my brother Andries had passed away.

Our eldest brother Jacobus was always the one who only watched our family grow in happiness and he never allowed any sorrow to touch our home. For where there were any tribulations or trouble, he would be there like a wishing star fulfilling everyone's wishes. Yet today he too kept himself busy within his medical journey of healing this world with his magical hands.

Big Papa's art studio is called Jacobus's Studio, named after the famous diarist of Kasteel Vrederic, Jacobus van Vrederic. It was the famous diarist who had restored and left all the portraits of our family members as he started our family tree. Later on, Big Papa had restored all of the portraits with his magical artist eyes and hands. Our art studio is near the famous canal Keizersgracht. The distance between the Keizersgracht and the Prinsengracht canal is about 350 meters, or about a four-minute walk.

We walked to the Mirrorless Hotel as we all needed a mental break. The walk was very nice as this is where Big Mama taught my brothers and me how to walk. She would bring us here and watch out for us. Jacobus was two years old when we were born so he too watched over us like a big brother.

I would see my family through touching all of them. I got to see my parents walk holding on to one another today. I expressed a sigh of relief watching them and felt like I was still in my childhood, when Big Mama and Big Papa would hold on to me and one another, it meant everything on this Earth would be all right.

We walked into a hotel that looked more like an amazing boutique style hotel rather than a majestical museum style hotel. The advertisement had retold a story that this was a majestical museum hotel. The hotel was rumored to have designer mirrors displayed all around the interior. The lobby was rumored to be like a house of mirrors, a maze where the guests would get lost.

We found nothing of that in the hotel. The hotel had no funky circus drapes covering the windows and doors. There were no mirrors brought back from traveling around the globe found here. I kept on searching for huge, haunted mirrors and yet only found some cheap portraits.

There were amazingly beautiful Delft potteries displayed around the lobby. It somehow felt like there were two different designers crossing one another. One was the fake magazine advertisement pictures that don't exist. Yet another one had olden values and had wanted to decorate with "old is gold" values.

I wondered why would they not advertise the hotel as what there is rather than trying to falsely advertise what there is not? This was a very nice boutique hotel. Yet I never said anything as the hotel manager greeted us.

Big Mama, however, was never the one known to keep her thoughts to herself. I watched Big Papa try to say something to her in sign language but he was not successful. He only smiled and let her be herself. He loved her attitude though as she was more Dutch than Big Papa. She spoke directly and never was a person to sweet-talk the subject.

She said out loud, "I wonder why the false advertisement? This is an amazing hotel but I thought we were going to walk into a casino or a maze or a circus or a house of mirrors. Where are the designer mirrors? The pictures are all false advertisement. Why were there pictures of different casinos from all over the world? This is amazing and beautiful. Why have you not advertised your own hotel? All you have to do is take pictures of your own hotel. You should add more Dutch artwork and some famous Dutch paintings."

The owners were working as their own managers and had a very nice reception desk. There was a huge stone fireplace that was now lit with candles for the summer months. The white curtains were all blowing in the breeze as the wraparound veranda had tourists sitting and enjoying the hot summer day.

Yet all the visitors seemed like visitors of the restaurant, rather than hotel guests. All the ceiling fans were on as were sweet romantic musical notes playing in the café near the lobby. Tea and biscuits were all displayed in the lobby for the visiting guests. I watched my Big Mama as she suddenly was so quiet. That was unlike her characteristics. Why did the hotel not have any overnight guests?

Big Papa said to Big Mama, "Are you all right? You look like you just saw ghosts or something. Why are you so cold and shivering?"

We followed her eyes as she was watching a huge grand piano in the lobby. The piano looked normal as no one was there yet as we observed it through the eyes of a psychic, we could all see the piano was playing on its own. Even this would not attract anyone's eyes as at times, pianos can be set to play automatically. It was the musical number the piano was playing, however, that made everyone in the room to get shivers. Even the restaurant guests had shivers for the piano was playing the sound of heartbeats. Everyone heard the sound get louder and louder.

The lights started to flicker and everyone in the restaurant started to leave. I knew now why there were no overnight guests. The hotel was rumored to be haunted yet now their deception of a haunted hotel instead of getting overnight guests, got rid of the overnight guests.

Then there was a voice that echoed in the whole room and said, "Mama's heart beats Andries."

Big Papa and Big Mama did not say anything as I knew they were used to these things and never let them take over life. They let these unnatural events be a part of life. I knew I too must be strong like my parents but I knew I was a very emotional man who would keep all his emotions hidden under the veil of my darkness. I wondered though if Big Mama was okay with what we heard.

For within close sight, it was hard for me to hide my emotions. Then the piano started to play a musical tune only known to our family members. A musical tune that was sung by the forbidden daughter of Kasteel Vrederic, the daughter who became the living love and breath of all the future lineages of the van Vrederic family members. The song she had written and sung always to all the children of Kasteel Vrederic was now being sung by someone with a childlike voice.

The voice said, "Mama, sing to me! I want to sleep now!"

I wondered how would someone else know the lyrics? We heard clearly the voice said, "Sing to me now!"

Then we all heard a woman started to sing to the demanding child, "Through Your Mama's Eyes."

THROUGH YOUR MAMA'S EYES

Through your Mama's eyes,

Come my baby

See this world,

Today, tomorrow,

And forever.

My dear baby,

See through your Mama's eyes,

The colorful night sky hides within her chest

Glowing lanterns as she sends them onto Earth

Like a lightning bolt to only guide you.

HEART BEATS YOUR NAME: VOWS FROM THE BEYOND

My revered baby,

See through your Mama's eyes,

The moon is your aunt

Who plays hide and seek

With you in the dark.

My sweet baby,

Watch through your Mama's eyes,

The stars above

Are standing guard

As they are your own knights guarding you.

My blessed baby,

See through your Mama's eyes,

The wind blows hard

So he can send you

All the flowers.

My angel baby,

Watch through your Mama's eyes,

The pouring rain is the waterfall

That quenches your thirst

Through her immortal drink.

My precious baby,
See through your Mama's eyes,
The thunder is the drum
Of musicians guiding
All to safety.

My enchanting baby,
Watch through your Mama's eyes,
The sun is your uncle
Who always greets you
At dawn.

My darling baby,
See through your Mama's eyes,
The seawater
Rises high to kiss
Your toes.

My cute baby,
See through your Mama's eyes,
The green grass grows
For you my child
So you never hurt your feet.

My loving baby,
Watch through your Mama's eyes,
The nights
Are not scary
Neither is the day.

My adorable baby,
Watch through your Mama's eyes,
All the birds are there
So they can sing sweet songs for you
Throughout the days and throughout the nights.

My cherished baby,
See through your Mama's eyes,
All your prayers will be blessed like miracles
As I shall always watch over you
And send you my immortal kisses.

My beloved baby,
See through your Mama's eyes,
This is a world where
All your dreams will be blessed and be true
As you go to sleep at night and awaken at dawn.

This lullaby

I sing for you

My treasured baby,

For remember to see this world,

THROUGH YOUR MAMA'S EYES.

I ran to the piano as it was playing while a sweet woman's voice was singing the lullaby to a young child. We all heard the woman and the child yet could not see anyone.

I asked the front desk, "What is going on? This song is copyrighted as it belongs to my family. No one has the right to sing it except the van Vrederic family members. Where did you get it from? And how dare you play it without our permission!"

The owners were an elderly couple in their late seventies. They were both very tall and very chubby with blond hair and blue eyes. The owners were shocked beyond words as they too looked like they just saw a ghost. My parents were upset as they had only sung the song to my brothers and me.

There was no way anyone else could have had the words or the musical notes which were written and sung by the daughter of the famous diarist, also known as the famous spirit of Kasteel Vrederic, Griet herself. To this day, all mothers including Big Mama had heard Griet sing the song to all arriving children of Kasteel Vrederic. I wondered what was going on here.

The hotel owners said, "We have to apologize for the current situation. We do advertise without a lie. This hotel is haunted and maybe the ghosts too know about your family songs."

Big Mama did not hold back as she too started to talk as she said, "I don't believe you don't lie. You have absolutely lied about your hotel and have given pictures of world-famous resorts while your hotel does not match the pictures."

She stopped and was watching directly at the piano and I knew was holding back her tears. Yet my brave mother held on to her tears and said, "Why do you call your hotel 'Mirrorless' if your advertisement is filled with mirrors? The name and the pictures advertising your hotel make no sense."

The owners were shocked at the question and tried to refrain from answering yet in a howling match replied, "Mirrors are linked to dark spirits and they can be used to bring back the dead or attract negative energy. Therefore, we don't have any mirrors in the hotel. Nor do we want to keep any. So we named the hotel 'Mirrorless Hotel.'"

My mother was watching the woman and did not refrain from answering. She watched the piano and saw more than she was willing to share yet only spoke with authority as a qualified psychic. Big Mama said, "As a psychic, I actually disagree. I believe mirrors reflect the person in front of the mirror. So if a positive person is in front it, then you would get all the positive energies from it. It's like predicting the future. I guess you all don't have any positive energies or vibes, within yourself or your hotel, so for you it's good not to have any mirrors as they also capture and transport souls, dead souls, and evil. I also wonder, would you remove all the water from this world as they too reflect energies similar to mirrors? Let's spread good not evil. Also, I would ask my husband to seek his lawyers to further investigate into you playing our family song and music in your hotel without permission."

I watched Big Papa watch Big Mama and knew there was no stopping Mama now. He just held on to a very petite Mama and watched her amusingly as he smiled and said nothing. His eyes were all his love for a woman who wouldn't keep anything in her mind.

I saw then Big Papa say, "You and your hotel, be it your hotel ghosts or your hotel guests, have violated copyright rules and I know my family lawyers would love to be in touch with you. Yet if you would allow us to investigate this situation on our own without any barricades from you the hotel owners, then we would come to an agreement and see what is going on."

I watched my parents talk with one another as they watched me and I told the owners, "Maybe we can advertise for your hotel as this is our family song and this hotel really must be haunted by unknown ghosts."

The owners were extremely happy rather than being upset and said, "We would be more than delighted to get any help from the van Vrederic family members. We are all fans of Erasmus van Phillip and you the famous blind painter. We are humbled to have you as our guests. You can investigate anything you so wish or choose to. We too want an end to the hauntings of this hotel."

The elderly man watched Big Mama and said, "I never advertise falsely but my daughter who hardly is here is also an artist and these images are all her paintings. We are not saying our hotel is like those places but actually our daughter has these artworks placed in all the rooms. Each room in the hotel has paintings of different places from around the globe. These we believe were hand created by our daughter. At least that's what she had told us, and we don't have any reason not to believe her. We must admit she had spent a lot of hours in each room with her computer. We never said they were her original creation. We are advertising different walls displayed in different rooms."

My Big Mama watched him and said, "It's false advertisement. Change the magazines and say in clear print those are paintings displayed in each room, not actual rooms."

He said, "On our next magazine, we will clarify it, as well as on our website."

I told the manager, "I have a gift for you and your hotel. I understand you buy paintings from around the globe and have wished to purchase something from our art studio. I have a painting I have created blindly in black and white for you."

The owners were extremely happy as they had tried to buy my black and white paintings for their hotel for a while and now they have me personally giving them a gift.

I told them, "I will leave it in our room. I believe we were given a family room as my parents too will come and go, while I take care of some business in town."

We were taken to our family room which had two bedrooms, and a living and dining area. I placed the painting on the table as I watched the paper that was wrapped around the painting open by itself. The painting had the woman in the frame watch over us as if she was alive and real, not a face in the frame.

It was then I heard a child's voice say, "Papa's heart beats Andries."

I watched the portrait as did my parents and thought who was the Papa the child was calling out to? Big Mama touched the painting and said, "It's my child who is calling from the beyond. I don't know what is going on, but he is calling us somehow."

Big Papa went near the painting and wiped his tears as he said, "We are reliving a parent's nightmare. My beloved wife, guide me so I too can control my emotions and be strong for all of you and myself."

Big Mama watched Big Papa and only spread her tears. He wiped her tears and said, "Thank you my love. Your tears have found my answers."

I was left alone as my parents left for home while I would be trying to investigate what happened to the missing mystical guest of the hotel. I kept on hearing the sound of heartbeats all night and I heard musical notes playing all around me. I realized these musical notes were not feared by my heart but accepted by my heartbeats as I knew the heartbeats of the strange night.

I heard a sweet voice say, "You are here my love. Tonight I am not scared as tonight, I shall sleep within your arms, the arms of my beloved. My heart beats musical notes in your name. From now on, until we unite shall be known as sweet and harmonious musical nights."

I watched the portrait I had created of my magical princess and whispered to her like the summer night's breeze, "My enchanting mystical princess of the night, why are you pulling me toward you? Is it because now you are forever alive within my eyes as I have lovingly captured you in the magical portrait?"

Dear beloved, tonight I am exhausted, as on this night, my parents went home crying for their son who has gone far away. Yet my mother believes he will rise like the magical phoenix and come back home to her. I believe in her words and I know both of you are coming home with us. For you with love, this is my fifth poem.

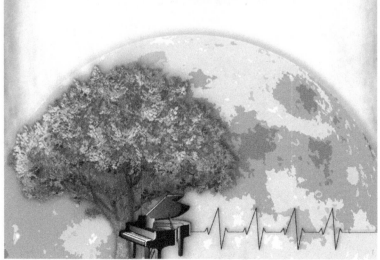

MAGICAL PORTRAIT

Like a mystical fog,

You entered my life

Through the door of passionate dreams.

You landed within my chest

As you were flying like a shooting star.

Your eyes brought with you

All the glowing hope of the full moon.

Within a hot summer's night,

Your whispers calmed

My burning scorching soul.

With your pouring tears,

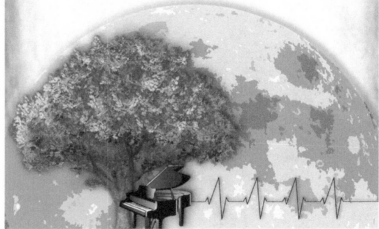

You filled my empty chest
And quenched my thirst.
With your nightly promises,
I have infinitely renewed
My vows of everlastingly yours.
With all the given and taken promises,
You have created a space
For yourself in my soul,
Yet do you not know,
You don't need to create
Any space in my chest,
For you are completely mine,
As I am forever only yours.

This promise I have framed
Tonight for you as I drew your face,
Our love and our vows
Of eternally yours in my,

MAGICAL PORTRAIT.

Signed: Antonius van Phillip

CHAPTER FIVE:

Musical Nights

"Sweet songs sung by a mother for a child or a beloved to a beloved cross time and tide as these songs keep the listener and the singer safe within the bond and safety of the musical nights."

Antonius van Phillip walks onto the veranda and finds a spirit Katelijne Snaaijer rocking a spirit baby boy and knows they are his wife and son, yet how?

The nightingales were all singing through a star-filled night. Canoes and boats on the Prinsengracht canal were filled with romantic couples trying to enjoy a blessed summer's night. All the sounds of the beautiful human tourists came to an end as the night skies were filled within musical notes of silence.

Children returned home to their parents. Couples returned home to recreate yet another romantic night. I could hear nothing but silence take over. Even the amazing moon was hiding behind a dark cloud, getting her sleep. Yet tonight I could not sleep. I wondered how many restless nights I would stay awake, not dreaming of you with my eyes closed. Yet I would still dream about you with my eyes open.

Why does it hurt so much I wonder as I don't even know you? I keep wondering, was life taken away from you even before life gave you a chance? I am here awake full of life, yet where are you sleeping so peacefully, all lifeless? I wonder if you have met my brother, for he too is sleeping under the majestical skies, while the moon keeps him guarded during the dark night and the sun bathes him during the day. Yet Big Mama said the clouds and the mystical breeze keep him comfortable through the days and the nights. Big Mama awaits his arrival as she believes in reincarnation and knows she found proof living through it herself.

I wonder why my heart beats for both of you, a woman I don't even know and my brother whom I miss so much yet still feel like he never left me. I will fight my destiny and gather the unknown answers to my quest. For I was taught by my parents, look into the heartbeats for they never lie.

My thoughts were broken as my cell phone rang. I picked up the phone and heard a very familiar calm and reassuring voice on the other side, the only voice that actually could calm me throughout the worst days of my life. My big brother Jacobus was on the phone.

He started to talk as I picked up the phone, "My dear brother, why on Earth are you staying at that hotel? Are you out of your mind? Mama just told me the complete details about the adventure ride you, Papa, and Mama went through. I will never judge you, however, there are some missing puzzle pieces of the picture only I know of. I repeat, Mama and Papa have no clue either. I really don't want you taking any risk over there as these people are dangerous."

I asked my big brother Jacobus, "What proof do you have and why am I even involved in this mystery? Yet I don't want to leave without finding out what happened to all of the young women who went missing. Also Jacobus, there is one particular woman my heartbeats keep calling upon. I feel like Aunt Marinda had prophesied about this one woman whose painting haunts me in a very thirst-quenching way. Hey big bro, I mean it also gives me a lot of pure pleasure and a somewhat uncomfortable but comfortable feeling in my chest. I am worried I might have fallen head over heels for a woman who might be dead."

I heard Jacobus was breathing very hard yet did not say anything as he always kept to himself. He did not share much of the burdens with anyone. It was his way of suffering for all yet not allowing the pain to spread to his loved ones.

He said, "Don't give up on your heartbeats. Remember follow your heartbeats, for heartbeats never lie. I believe you are head over heels in love with a woman you think is dead. Yet why would that prevent you from loving her? Remember bro, love is immortal even though life is not. Don't allow any negative thoughts to take over your love for your beloved."

I always knew Jacobus would think deep about love. For we all knew the eternal love story of Jacobus van Vrederic and his beloved wife Margriete van Wijck. I knew very well he would never look at another woman in any of his reincarnated forms but wait for his beloved Margriete.

Jacobus then said, "Somehow I believe you are being led to the answers by the rhythm of the musical heartbeats. Don't give up on them for I have not given up on anyone. I promise you too shall be gifted with answers from the beyond. I know Mama and Papa call them vows from the beyond. Believe in them and all shall be all right. Yet please do not ever trust the hotel owners or their daughter, who is believed to be evil incarnate."

I listened to my brother who was only two years older than myself. Yet he was very wise, as if he had traveled time and knew so much more than what even historians have written down as historical facts. I knew I could not ask, for Jacobus will share with me when it is time.

I only told him, "I love you, big brother, and I will follow the heartbeats as these are my vows from the beyond. Yet did you know I had the feeling this woman holds my twin flame's soul? She might be dead or she might be alive, still I don't know but it feels like I hold her life in my hands like a thread that ties us in a knot."

Jacobus laughed and said, "Life is a thread held on to by one another through memories, some that were created, some that will be created, and some that are lost. Yet life in itself is a wagon which only moves forward unless you can get on the wagon of dreams. For then, you can time travel and look into what really had happened. Believe in your heartbeats my brother. They will take you in the right direction. Also keep an eye out for Mama. She is a psychic so she knows what I have not said yet, or what you all have not found out as of yet."

I listened to him and said, "Is this my doctor brother talking or is this Big Mama talking through him? Jumping onto the wagon of dreams sounds like the train our parents had traveled upon as they found one another. Mama's heart beats my name, so she is my first love."

Jacobus laughed aloud for a while as he said, "Actually, Mama's heartbeats her three sons, as our hearts beat for both Mama and Papa."

I told him, "Forever eternally I want to be born in this mother and father's embrace."

Jacobus then said, "Also believe in miracles my brother, a lesson taught by our parents should never be forgotten. No doctor or scientist in my own body would ever argue with that theory as I was there to unite them even before my birth. Maybe there is someone else who wants to help his parents or others through the mystical door of dreams."

We both laughed as our family history was magical and even though not proven by science, at least it can't be denied by science as we are all living proof.

I told him, "I am a patient man who has lived in the dark patiently. Now I will patiently wait in the daylight to find out the dark truth of the hidden nights. For I will find out who is behind all the murders happening in the dark."

Jacobus asked me, "How do you know the murders are happening in the dark?"

I told him, "All the portraits were made in the dark. The sketches were actually pictures taken on a camera and then altered on the computer to look like handmade portraits. I guess they were to either fool the police or mock the girls. Either way, the culprit is hiding in the dark. The artist is a heartless criminal who enjoys watching others suffer for his or her own pleasure. A very sick person who is hiding in the dark. I will catch him or her, as I lived in the dark."

Jacobus only said, "Follow the heartbeats. They will lead you to your answers. I will come and join you as soon as I finish up on some transplant surgeries I must complete to save as many lives as possible. My oath as a doctor comes first."

I told him, "Dear brother, remember life is a gift and must end at the time allocated to end. You can do your best but you too are a human who needs to take a break."

He said, "Take care my brother and I shall never let any one of my family members go, not a single one. For if they are gone, then I must find a way out for them to return."

I knew who he was talking about. He was thinking about our brother Andries. I knew my family believed in reincarnation but somehow, I had a feeling my big brother believed in miracles more than the doctor in him would admit. Yet here I am living with a miracle performed by my two brothers.

A singing voice got my attention, as it was coming from within my suite. I wondered if Big Mama and Big Papa had returned. So I walked to the living room area to check on them. There was the moon streaming in through the open veranda left open probably by my mother. I walked to the veranda and saw there was a woman sitting on a rocking chair with a baby on her lap. She watched me and told me to not say anything as she must sing the child to sleep.

She then sang the same lullaby my family ancestors were singing for generations. A gift left by a spirit mother for her child, sixteenth-century daughter Griet had left it for her daughter, Margriete 'Rietje' Jacobus Peters, granddaughter of Jacobus van Vrederic. This gift was given to us by Jacobus van Vrederic in one of his famous diaries known as *Evermore Beloved: I Shall Never Let You Go.*

I then heard the sound of heartbeats playing on a piano. It was so soothing as if I knew the heartbeats so well. It did not frighten me yet made a warm feeling within my chest. I knew I should not approach the mother, who was so lovingly hugging and singing to her son.

She said, "Antonius, help us please. We have been waiting for you. Won't you please find us and take us home? Also I love the moonlit nights, as it's then I can see you even in the dark. I love you my beloved. Please don't forget me or our son."

I saw in the bright moon covered veranda was the woman I had sketched in black and white. I left the portrait on top of the living room fireplace as a gift for the host. Yet here she was in front of me in color. Her brown hair landed upon her shoulders. Her brown eyes were busy deep in her own thoughts.

A woman about five feet, eight inches tall. I could tell she was of Dutch origin. Yet she looked very small and fragile. I went beyond what a normal person would do and stood closer to her. She looked a little faded as if she was transparent yet somehow, she also looked very real.

I then just had to ask her who she was and I said, "Who are you? Why do I see you in my dreams? Why is it now you are sitting in my hotel room with a child? I really need to know the answers as I believe you and I have something that ties us to one another. If you too believe we have something that binds us together, then please help me. I don't know who else to ask or go to for help. I know you must somehow be related to Kasteel Vrederic and me, for otherwise you would not have known this song."

She watched me for a while and smiled so sweetly. I knew now she was mesmerizing me.

I said out loud, "Oh my God, I am being mesmerized by the most beautiful woman on or beyond this Earth. Now Big Mama had said not to ever rush and fall in love, but let love come to you. Unlike any other mothers who try to set up their children, our mother always sent all the girls running away from our home. Now are you saying I am falling in love with a spirit woman, instead of a physical woman? Oh yes, my mother had interrogated women even harder than an army inquiry."

She started to cry and she watched me and said, "I am scared. Why am I in this stage? Are you saying I am dead? Yet I had seen myself talking with your brother Jacobus. He promised me I will be all right. Then how are you saying I am dead? If I am dead, then how did I have your son? I know I have been with you for so long, for the last three years. Yet I can't remember anything beyond that. I always thought we fell madly in love with one another. I don't know where you go during the day yet I get to see you during the nights. Please help us."

A crying woman whom I had no clue as to who she was, said she is my wife and she was holding on to our son who too looked like a spirit. I did not know what to think but I needed Big Mama and Big Papa to help me. Yet I somehow did not want them to be worried about all of this, until I could figure out more of the story myself.

I told her, "I will help you and I shall never let you go or fall prey to anyone. I promise I will find a way to help you somehow, even if it is my last breath."

She watched me and said, "How could you take your last breath as I am still breathing? It's because my son is breathing inside of me. It's the musical heartbeat that unites us my love. For as long as I have my heartbeats, you shall always be mine as I will never let go of our son. His heartbeats are my heartbeats and his love for you and me shall always hold us in unity throughout eternity. These are my vows from the beyond as even though we are separated by a breath, our son keeps us breathing."

That one night was so long and yet I never wanted the night to end. I kept on thinking my beautiful self-proclaimed spirit wife was sleeping on a swing as the moon's glorious light was reflecting on her face.

At all times, she kept on saying, "My beloved son, you are my glowing hope that shall always shine and be safe within this mother's womb."

The heartbeats that kept on singing all night were so pleasant as I was actually comforted by the mystical sound. Somehow, I knew I must talk with Jacobus about how the woman died or if she did die or where she was. Until then, I knew I must keep the heartbeats singing.

It was as if within these heartbeats was tied my entire existence. Tonight though, I let the musical heartbeats sing sweet songs to comfort my heart. I knew as long as my heart beats so shall theirs. I prayed to my Lord, let all nights be sweet, magical, musical nights.

Dear cherished, tonight I had a
magical night with you. If you do
remember or not, I shall treasure these
memories eternally. This is my sixth
poem written with all my love for my
darling, my love, only for you.

MUSICAL NIGHTS

The singing nightingales
Are busy tonight as they join
The musical stars of the night
Who are joined by the shooting stars

Who are dancing as they have found
Their friend thunder to join the beats,
Who also has found the charming winds
To join as flutes of the night,
As they have found
The pouring summer rain
To be a part of the nightly concerts.
They celebrate as all watch
Twin flames rise again and again
From burning ashes.
All are rejoicing tonight
For you and I have found
One another spiritually.

For from tonight and eternally,
Let all our nights be known to
You and me as the magical,

MUSICAL NIGHTS.

Signed: Antonius van Phillip

CHAPTER SIX:

Painter's Murdered Models

"A culprit captures his hatred, his anger, and his rage within his framed artwork. Yet a sacred artist can see through the fog and unmask the masked painter and the painter's murdered models."

Katelijne Snaaijer and the baby boy guide Antonius van Phillip to the hotel cellar.

awn broke through the sweet musical night as the morning sun's rays streamed in through to my room. I saw no sign of my previous night's guests. The amazingly beautiful, innocent deep brown eyes that gazed at me with all her trust and love was nowhere to be found. The endearing baby boy who held on to his mother and robbed my sleep and all my fatherly love, too was missing. All I had was the black and white portrait I had created not copying the original painting that was given to me but of how I saw my mystical princess in my dreams, a very frightened woman who kept calling on me for help.

All night, I had heard the sweet musical heartbeats of the mother and son. Yet in the vivid daylight, I felt so lonely and I was immersed in a strange emotional bond with the two people I presumed to be dead. Then why does my heart beat your name my supernatural princess and my little enchanting prince?

The door of my hotel suite opened as I could smell my mother enter. I knew elegance, charm, and grace followed my mother at all times. It is strange how being blind had given me my sixth sense. Yet I knew even my brothers know when she is around.

All the sadness and grief in the world evaporate just when I see the woman who had taken my inner soul away as she taught me to walk. The story goes I learned to crawl and then walk just by following her smell. I could find her any day and any night, just by following the bond of love.

My mother is five feet, four inches tall. Her olive skin tone is like myself and my twin brother's. No one ever realized she is not my biological mother. My Big Mama's magical hair is raven black as it always blows in the wind. I would hold on to my mother's hair when I got scared hearing the thunder that came after the warning of the lightning which I could not see.

She walked in and said, "Mama's heart beats my sons' names, and how could I eat breakfast knowing one of my sons is sleeping in a room probably haunted by a spirit woman? Oh well, dear woman, you know my son is very handsome so do stay far away until I approve you, ghost or human, it really does not bother me."

I started to laugh at my mother's comments, as I watched Big Papa with his elegant tall stature of six feet and five inches, very pale European skin tone, light brown hair, and gray-blue eyes follow my very petite Indian Big Mama. Wherever they went, the room would start glowing with pure love. Yet upon hearing Big Mama's comments, Big Papa broke into a fit of laughter as he knew Big Mama said she would not give up on her Indian ways of thinking and would look out for a good daughter-in-law.

We, the three brothers, were told from childhood that Mama has to approve a woman even before we start to date. So all the girls and women would actually stay far away after meeting Big Mama as she had introduced all to the spirits of Kasteel Vrederic first. She would let everyone know they would be watched over by the spirits at all time. The women and girls at our young age had all run in the opposite direction.

Big Papa said, "We must begin early as we need to find out the mystery behind the portraits before your mother gets you wedded with a spirit or a woman, who may or may not even be dead. We know most of the women painted in the portraits recovered by the police were found dead, yet some of the faces were disfigured as if someone hated either the women or how they looked. As an artist, you would agree you only disfigure a face when you hate the person. So, I wonder why or who is doing it."

I told Papa what had happened last night. We all knew Mama knows so much more than she was saying. She watched me and said, "I have seen dreams you will fall in love with a spirit yet somehow if your love can survive the test of time and tide, then she will not be a spirit anymore. I also know you have a lot of questions but I can't answer what is not known to the visible eyes. Yet I had seen something about your brother Jacobus. For in my dreams, I had kissed my son's hands and told him may his hands be blessed throughout eternity."

I told Mama and Papa, "Jacobus is coming soon. He has asked me to find out all I could about the woman before he arrives as then he will see how his found pieces of the puzzle complete the mystery."

We had a huge Indian and Dutch breakfast of fresh homemade roti, paratha, aloo matar, and sabzee sent by my Nani. I also saw on the table was fresh baked bread with butter. We also had appelstroop, hazelnut-chocolate spread, and sweet sprinkles which we call hagelslag. I watched Big Papa eat the roti and paratha with the curries as I did, yet Big Mama had the typical Dutch breakfast.

She then said, "I love a Dutch breakfast. I married a Dutchman as I fell madly in love with him, his food, his country, and his culture. I can have hagelslag every day."

We all went in different directions to gather all the information we could from the hotel to which the crimes were linked. I knew for some reason I needed to find out who the painter of these portraits was. For all of the paintings were gifted to this one hotel and they were all taken to Big Papa's art studio as it became a police case. The culprit had done a favor to the owners as all reviews or news, even negative news, had brought them customers from all over the world.

I realized all the women were of different races and cultures. So the artist had to be connected to all the victims across the world. If we could follow the evidence through the globe, then we should find out who the culprit was. The victims were all women and the portraits capture very frightened women who look like they just saw the Angel of Death. Yet I couldn't understand why all the paintings somehow landed upon this hotel.

I met with the owner Mr. Luyt Bakker and Mrs. Livina Bakker-Beenhouwer as they offered me fresh fruits and breakfast. I told them, "I really appreciate the breakfast but my mother is here and I can't disappoint her, as she and my grandmother make the world's best food which I will eat even if I am full. It's made with love and made by the world's best cooks. I had breakfast, thank you."

They both laughed and understood my dilemma. I went straight to the point and asked, "Mr. and Mrs. Bakker, I would like to visit the storage room or cellar where all of the portraits were found. I understand the police have informed you to help us with everything we need as we are trying to only help them. In this particular case, my family is involved as my brother had tried to save one victim. I believe he could not save her, yet I know we want to do something for her."

Livina said, "I know what we must do, yet one thing you must understand is we were not involved in any of the crimes. I found the portraits in my cellar and they were being hung in different rooms of our hotel. I personally called the police and informed them I did not order the portraits as I imagined they were left for Jacobus's Studio. I had sent them to the art studio and it is then Erasmus van Phillip had sent them to the police."

I watched her as she was speaking and again my sixth sense was saying she was telling the truth. She was nervous and shaking yet there was truth and fear flowing within her chest. I then tried to observe her husband.

I saw he had tears falling from his eyes as he said, "I feel guilty I loved having the portraits as they brought us customers. People came to see our hotel just to see if the murders had happened here. The rooms the paintings were hung in had spiked in price as people wanted to pay more money. Yet the last painting had brought my consciousness back into my soul which I never knew I even had."

I watched my parents walk in and they were just observing us talk as they helped themselves to freshly brewed coffee. My mother, however, brought me a fresh cup of coffee. She said, "Antonius have some coffee, I know you love coffee."

I knew my mother will always be herself even in front of people the police are thinking to be the main suspects.

My mother again said, "Who is the amazing painter of this hotel? I can see the world through the art collection you have displayed around the hotel. I am assuming you two are world travelers."

They were shocked at her words and both of them were numb for a while. Livina said, "We never stepped outside of this country. We don't have time to travel, and we have our hotel here, so why should we travel?"

I told them, "I understand you have a hotel in Tennessee in the USA. You have another one in Paris, France. You also have another one in Bali, Indonesia. How did you open hotels around the globe without franchising them out, but completely keeping them in your name without leaving the country?"

They both laughed and again Livina spoke, "Our daughter Aideen manages all of our hotels. She loves traveling and hiring local people. She loves interviewing them and tries to give women a chance as she believes in women's rights. She stays in a place just long enough to set up the hotel and then moves on to the next one. We are blessed she is very smart."

I watched the parents talk with pride as they spoke about their child. I knew the police must have investigated all of this. Yet what was the missing puzzle piece they needed an artist to check out?

I asked her directly, "Aideen must be very confident as she did so well. I am presuming she studied in the Netherlands. Which university did she go to?"

It was strange as Luyt said, "She went to Erasmus University. She did her bachelor's degree in International Business Administration. After university, in her own time she trained herself to become a graphic designer all by herself. She told us that was because she wanted to create artwork on the computer. Yet I don't know why our daughter's name is even being brought into this as she is never here, but always busy traveling."

I watched my parents still walking around the library we were talking within. I realized Big Papa was amused by the collection of books, yet I wondered what Big Mama was doing. I then saw Big Mama touch a painting that was set on the side table by the owners. She walked to it as I saw in the room was my mystical princess standing at the corner of the small table, holding on to the hands of a child of about two years old.

He looked strangely familiar as I walked toward them yet Big Mama held on to my hands and prevented me from going to them. Big Mama said, "Who painted this picture of you two? It looks so real, like you are watching over us from within the frame. I am assuming the artist did this with her hands as a portrait."

They were proud parents as they glowed with pride and again, I heard Livina say, "Our daughter did that on a computer. It's not a painting but a picture. She is a self-proclaimed artist who never shares her identity as an artist. She does it for fun."

I then was released by my mother as I walked to the portrait and gasped in amusement. As an artist, I could guarantee and say it was the same artist. All the women who were pictured, the paintings were forged to look like they were painted by hand. They were done by the same artist. I felt strange as I knew the fake finger paintings like a real fingerprint led us to the con artist.

All the places she had traveled to and opened a hotel in were where all the victims were found. Yet no one could even put her at the place of the murder or link her to the victims. I wondered why, yet then how could we do what others have failed? I saw the child standing at the corner of the room as the sound of the heartbeats played on the piano. I knew we would be able to solve this because we had this child who would help.

The police had gone over her details yet she was never found at the place of the murder yet as an artist, I knew the picture within the frame in my hands and the portraits recovered were all done by the same artist who had fooled all and wanted to fool all.

It was amazingly strange as I heard the little boy say, "Papa, help please. I want to be born as my heart beats her name."

I only watched them and said, "Your daughter can't be a suspect as she is always traveling. Yet it is so strange the victims too are traveling or it just happens they too are following your daughter. I wonder is your daughter following them or they are following her? Yet there is no proof of anything but the con artist will be exposed by me, the blind artist. As I have lived in the dark all my life, I can see everything even though you might be hiding in the dark."

Livina watched me and said, "I know there is no way my daughter would have anything to do with all of these artworks as she is not even a portrait artist. She just takes pictures."

I went to the cellar that night and it was there I saw more artworks left by the painter who was not even an artist yet left more of her fingerprints all over her art studio. As I walked into the dark cellar, I again watched a mother and a son just watching over me. I followed their gaze as they showed me a specific spot they both stood upon.

There was a trap door under them. I went to the spot and they moved over. I lifted the trap door trying to make sure no one was watching over me. I had been shown a specific cellar but not this one. I followed my mystical princess and came in here. A loud bang got me so freaked out that I jumped over and saw Big Mama and Big Papa standing there.

I asked them, "Why have you two not gone home but are following me? What if the owners find out? Did you two think what if they are involved in these murders?"

Big Mama said, "They are not involved in the murders. They are just innocent parents who have been placed in a trap. I believe they too want answers as they have lost their lifetime of good reputation. The couple actually never had any children of their own. As a childless couple who wanted a baby so much, they happily adopted a young child. The girl never got into any trouble nor did she have any boyfriends nor husbands. She is forty years old and has a good reputation herself."

Big Mama watched the two spirits just standing there and said, "I still believe the girl has a hidden identity. As a psychic, I feel she has a dual identity of some kind. I might be wrong but we need to figure out if she is the culprit, then how did she do all of this without even being suspected by anyone?"

Then in front of us, the hidden trap door just opened on its own. My parents were not shocked or scared like normal parents would be. Yet this was like their normal day and events as living in Kasteel Vrederic, my family learned to accept everything as another day's events.

I saw there under the trap door was a dark room we all walked into. The room in the cellar felt like a photo printing studio and a computer lab. I watched there were life-size mirrors all around the room. The mirrors were all covered with black sheets. The whole room was like a dark painter's dark room. Then I watched the little boy start to dig a hole in the middle of the room with his tiny hands. I walked over as did Big Mama and that's when I knew she too saw them. All I saw were tears that betrayed the emotions of my Big Mama and myself.

She kissed my head and said, "I carried you for over two years as you refused to walk, so I know my son takes after me."

I kissed my mother's head back and saw Big Papa watching over us as he too started to dig the floor which was unfinished and had gravel on just one spot. After digging for a while, we found an old chest which had inscribed on top of it, *Painter's Murdered Models*.

My beloved twin flame, it was so painful
to witness art being used as a criminal's
game plan or escape route or even
pleasure. Yet I promise I shall always
protect you from their hands. Again
tonight, I have written my seventh poem
just for you.

PAINTER'S MURDERED MODELS

Framed within a portrait,
I have kept you to remind myself
You are mine as I am only yours.

Gently within my chest,

I shall forever

Hold you tucked away

Within my eternal love

And affection.

You will be held in my chest,

For close within my warm chest,

You will hear my heartbeats

And know I am your beloved.

Forever my love,

My beloved,

Stay within my soul

As I am lonely

During the cold nights.

I am thirsty for you

During the summer nights.

And forever and always,

I, the beloved,

Shall hold and protect you

From all evil of the nights.

I shall keep you sheltered safely

Within my complete soul

As you are my twin soul

And I am yours.

So I promise

You shall never

Be a part of
The evil deceiving

PAINTER'S MURDERED MODELS.

Signed: Antonius van Phillip

CHAPTER SEVEN:

Unravel The Murder Mystery

"Solving a mystery in your mind is the first step, yet how does one cross it in reality? The answer lies with each step taken to finish the journey, as at the end of the bridge, the answer is found to unravel the murder mystery."

Katelijne Snaaijer and the baby boy guide the van Phillip family to the evidence chest buried in the hotel cellar.

The dark cloudy night seemed to have taken over our small world tonight. The roaring thunders and heavy pouring rain kept our investigation hidden within Mother Nature's musical concert of the night. Big Mama heard something as she was guarding the trap door.

We stopped everything and stayed quietly in the dark hidden cellar of the Mirrorless Hotel. In a few seconds, the sound became even clearer as now it was not just slow tap dancing but heavy footsteps. Then we heard voices and knew there was more than one person coming toward us. My brave Big Mama jumped into Big Papa's chest. She closed her eyes and hid herself in his chest.

She said in a demanding voice, "Erasmus, hide me now! I am scared they will find us and murder all of us."

Big Papa said, "Sweetheart, don't worry! You are forever hidden in my chest. I had never let you go. I shall never let you go."

I watched my parents and could not help myself but love them even more as I told them, "We will all be all right Mama. Just have faith for I know you already know the end result as you had written this in your dream diaries. Yet I understand we must choose our own path, which will then decide the end result. Nonetheless, I know we will choose the right path."

Big Mama said, "Yes and I want the end result to be in your Big Papa's chest with my three boys. All three of you in my chest."

I watched Big Papa kiss her head as we all knew that was going to be impossible. Yet neither did he say anything nor did I. It was then I watched my spirit mystical princess wipe her tears as she watched her son watching Big Mama and even he too cried.

He kept on watching Big Mama and pulled his mother to go near her. Yet the woman just stood there, as if she was stuck somewhere in an oblivious world. The child too seemed weaker than before as I knew they were fighting against time.

The strangest thing was the child was crying for Big Mama and her pain. He wanted to run toward Big Mama but was not able to. Then strangely I thought I heard him say in a baby voice, "Big Mama's heart beats my name."

Nothing made any sense to me but I kept quiet. I thought they were probably able to hear and see all of us, like I know Big Mama too saw them. I knew I was falling head over heels for the woman who had so many times reassured me I was her twin flame. I knew it was true for somewhere in my inner soul, I kept on calling for her and the baby boy.

I kept on repeating to myself, I must be strong and not worry about the painter in the dark as I am a painter who had painted everything from the dark. I will catch her in her own games as soon as my big brother Jacobus can give me some more information which he was not willing to share on the phone. Yet I wondered how did he know this woman? I knew the answers were hidden with the wagon of time.

I could not stay here and waste time so I tried to follow the sounds. I realized I had an advantage because I lived in the dark all of my life. I got up and took my walking cane I still carry even with sight. I walked with it and tried to find air. I felt there was a draft of cold air coming in from somewhere. I could feel it through my sixth sense, which normally one would ignore.

Big Mama said, "I can hear the hotel owners walking above our heads. It's their voices I hear. Listen carefully and you will hear her too."

I tried to listen to the words as soon it was clear, and I knew people were coming closer to us.

Luyt was talking to his wife, "If you or your daughter are involved in any of these murders, I will be the first one to call the cops on you. I don't trust our daughter. Her anger, jealousy, and rage always worry me. I pray she is not involved and you are not protecting a criminal."

Surprisingly there were no sounds of a wife arguing back or a mother trying to protect her daughter by arguing back. Then the footsteps were coming closer toward us. I knew we must find a way out of here without being noticed by anyone. Yet I only worried how we do this.

Then Livina said, "I can't believe you are always blaming me for your daughter. You spoiled her rotten. All the money you just handed over to her to do as she pleases. I knew who the child was. I knew who the young woman I raised was. Yet this forty-year-old woman that came home after ten years of being missing, I don't know. She completed international hotels without our permission. I was happy with this one hotel. She created the chain, I don't want to be linked to anyway. I still wonder how she got the money to do all of these for our one hotel keeps us floating on the ground but did not give us that kind of money."

I could not see them but thought he must be feeling guilty for blaming her as there were no sounds but just sniffles from crying.

Then Livina said, "Daughter or no daughter, if she is somehow involved in these horrific crimes, I will personally send her to a lifetime of imprisonment. I only hope she is not the horrific killer who has taken the lives of so many innocent women. She is only one daughter but what about all the other daughters who were taken away from their family members too early. No sweetheart, I don't blame you or myself but I only blame the woman our child had become, as how could we have missed it? Also if she is not the culprit, then I will always hate myself for bringing the police into this and maybe place our only child in danger. I want to see what she had hidden or done in that cellar. She had spent days and nights in front of the mirrors. Why were there so many mirrors all over her rooms anyway?"

Luyt said to his wife, "Did you not hear what the famous psychic Anadhi Newhouse van Phillip had said? She said one can trap evil spirits in the mirrors, so your daughter must have wanted to trap spirits or somehow get powers or something through the mirrors."

We got up with great haste and knew we must find a way out of here, however, I wondered why did she have all of these mirrors, covered in black cloaks? I knew Big Mama knew the answer as it showed on her fearful face. I kept on thinking there must be some hidden secret that is in front of us but maybe I will find it in the portraits upon closer inspection.

I thought Big Mama had told us, one could frame a life through a portrait yet in a mirror, you could see the truth, not the painter's vision of you. So it meant Aideen wanted to trap the beauty of others in her mirror, but not see her own ugly face. Hence, she covered the mirrors with black cloaks. Then, I was shocked as the next conversion reached my ears.

Livina said to her husband, "Aideen had hired Katelijne Snaaijer, the sweet and beautiful girl to be our manager and help us out with the hotel. The poor girl needed a place to stay and we needed a helping hand. The money was too much for us to pay as we did our own work. Yet I never said anything as I thought Aideen was probably trying to help the young woman. She was so beautiful and so kind to everyone. I felt we had two daughters rather than just an employee. I lied to the police and told them I don't know what had happened to her as it's not our business when an employee quits. Yet I know she was in the cellar with Aideen. When the poor girl won the most beautiful woman portrait contest which Aideen participated in yet lost, Aideen invited her over. She hired Katelijne and got everyone to like her. Then what had happened?"

Livina stopped talking as if she needed some time to think or was afraid of something yet tried to act normal. I knew she knew much more than she was sharing yet said nothing but just wanted to hear what she had to say.

Livina continued, "Katelijne was with all the dead women found in the graveyard. What had happened? Did Aideen do anything to her? I can't even walk into the cellar in fear of finding some hidden skeletons. By God, I remember Aideen had gotten furious as she had told the poor girl to repeat a thousand times she was ugly and Aideen was beautiful. Oh God, she had used those mirrors to stare at herself, but why? I assumed it was just childish deeds that would pass."

That's when we heard a sound coming from somewhere else. I walked closer toward the draft of air as Big Papa and Big Mama came closer toward me. We all followed the draft and the streaming light that was coming in from somewhere. I realized I was trained as a blind person to notice the simple flickering light that had touched my sixth sense.

Another trap door had opened as we saw an elderly man with a full beard looking at us. His hair blew in the wind. The full moon with her glory peeked from beneath the clouds and was shining on his back. He made a gesture to not talk as he told us with his hands to only follow him.

While we followed him out of the cellar, we saw we had actually landed upon a graveyard. The place felt cold and eerie even though there were evergreens, wooden benches, and fresh flowers filling the grounds. There was a swing hung from an English oak tree, swinging in the air.

On the swing was a name carved with a lot of love hearts that said, "Jantje Snaaijer, loving wife of Ghileyn Snaaijer and loving mother of Katelijne Snaaijer, never will you be too far away from us as wherever you are physically or spiritually, you are forever with us."

We walked a short distance on a very rainy and foggy night. Then we came near a church where all the lights were turned off. Yet we walked past the church to a small cottage by the church. Our rescuer had a key and let us in.

No one talked while we walked into the very small yet peaceful cottage. The small home was very nicely furnished with all the basic necessities of life. I assumed this was the private cottage of the church preacher who was from Loppersum, Groningen.

The small kitchen had a kettle on top of the stove that was turned on to make a fresh pot of tea. Fresh baked bread was taken out from the oven and was sliced up and set on the table. I watched the man who rescued us as he was busy making tea, biscuits, and fresh baked bread for his guests.

His seventy-year-old hands were very swift and precise, as he knew what he was doing.

He finally spoke, "Please help yourselves. I am Ghileyn Snaaijer, the preacher of this church. The swing we walked by was in memory of my deceased wife, which my daughter and I had made. I would hope you understand my daughter is my life and I married her mother when she was about one year old. She is not my biological child, yet I am her father. I taught her to walk and talk. I raised her alone after my wife had passed away from breast cancer, when Katelijne was only a toddler."

I knew he wanted to say so much yet he did not know how to get it out of his mind into words. I have the same problem. I can think out exactly what I want to say yet getting it out in words was always hard. I watched Big Mama get up and open the small fridge as she only followed the man with her eyes. She got the cream out and poured a generous amount for herself. Big Papa smiled to himself and tried to keep cool as we watched my mother get the jar of biscuits and take out a generous amount. She placed them on the plate for everyone to share.

Big Mama said, "I am so glad you welcomed us into your home. I hope you don't mind, I can't take one biscuit per person as per Dutch tradition. I actually had taken the whole plate when my mother-in-law was passing on one biscuit per person. I realized later it was Dutch culture, yet I like to bring some American and Indian cultures blended into my Dutch land, I call the land of my dreams. It always bothers me what if I want more than one biscuit?"

Big Papa burst into a laughter as did the preacher and I was shocked so did I. Big Papa kissed my mother's head and watched her so lovingly. The cold ice was broken in between us as everyone was so much more relaxed.

I told the preacher, "I shall forever be grateful to you for saving our honor and grace, maybe even our life. I don't know how you arrived there in the nick of time as we really needed a way out."

He watched all of us and asked, "What were you doing there in the dark? It's not a secret who you guys are. Everyone in the neighborhood knows the blind painter is staying at the Mirrorless Hotel. I really don't think it helps when he is accompanied by his famous father and the famous psychic author mother either, especially after that hotel hired my daughter deceitfully and then my child went missing for months. She was found taped, grogged, raped, and left out in the graveyard next to her mother's grave, dead."

He got up and watched the graveyard not too far from his view. I watched again my beautiful mystical princess appear with her son. As I saw the woman, Big Mama jumped up and watched the mother and son in astonishment. Nothing could be kept in secrecy from my mother nor could she keep anything in her mind.

She said, "Erasmus, in my knowledge, dead people can only come back to the places they were in life. Yet how is she traveling to this place then?"

She then watched the boy and wanted to say something but the boy watched Big Mama and placed a finger on his lips. He shook his head and told her to not say anything. Mama stopped herself, and she again started to cry as she knew something none of us knew.

I heard a heartbeat and the piano in the church next door was playing on its own. The sweet sound was of a heartbeat that was waking up all the dead and the sleeping nightly souls. The sound was actually comforting in a strange way. The sound kept getting louder and louder as it was warning us we must hurry.

The preacher said, "The painting you have followed and the police are investigating is of the same woman who was found dead in the grave. She was and shall always be my only child. Yes, everyone reminds me she was my wife's daughter, yet in our home and in my life, she is my child and nothing can change that. I will find out what had happened to her, as I don't believe my daughter was raped by random goons and was left bleeding in the graveyard to be dead for nothing."

Ghileyn stopped talking and just exhaled his stress out. I realized he had a lot of hidden pain in his inner chest he needed to get out. We all allowed him his needed time and waited for him to recollect his thoughts.

After inhaling and exhaling for a while, he continued, "I know that hotel and its owners and their horrendous and atrocious daughter had something to do with my daughter's murder. I won't die in peace until I find out. The hotel owner's daughter is all evil, and I believe the grounds she walks on becomes a graveyard. She has a cold and chilling ambiance around her, like she is the succubus, the she-devil herself."

He walked to the window and watched the graveyard outside for a while and then he said, "Jacobus Vrederic van Phillip, your son, was my daughter's doctor. She had a heart murmur from birth that needed immediate treatment. He was treating her for a few months as she was approached by this hotel. As a poor man, I could not pay Dr. Jacobus, and as a kind man, he never charged us for her treatment. Yet my daughter Katelijne wanted to pay him back so she accepted the job offer at that horrific devil's den. She was very happy as the extra money helped her mental situation."

The honorable preacher took another break as he now looked much older than he really was. I wondered how he had held on to all of his emotions without sharing with anyone for so long. Big Papa and Big Mama too remained quiet and just held on to one another throughout the whole nightmare.

The preacher continued his thought, "Before she even began working for the hotel, she was approached by an art museum from Paris, where they wanted to showcase international portraits of beautiful women from around the globe. She had accepted the offer as the money offered was something we needed to pay off her medical bills. After she started to work for the hotel, she reassured me the hotel owners were nice and she liked working with them. She did say she felt an unnerving discomfort around the daughter. Yet my innocent child was naïve."

I observed the preacher who was in his late seventies was actually shaking and panic-stricken by the memories. I knew he was still living in the past. He was about six feet, five inches tall, and of European descent. He had a full beard that had not seen any razors for a while. The preacher had shoulder length gray and brown hair. His eyes were dark blue like the ocean. He also had a bad knee as every time he walked, he held his leg in a way I knew he was in pain.

My parents and I never asked him if his daughter's medical condition was fixed or not. We knew even Jacobus wouldn't say anything for she was his patient. Jacobus, a heart surgeon and also an eye surgeon, now performs unique body organ transplant surgeries worldwide. My brother is the world's number one miracle doctor, and he is known as the doctor with magical hands.

The preacher started to talk again as he said, "My daughter won the portrait competition the hotel owners' evil daughter had entered yet lost. I knew that evil woman entered so many competitions. She had not won any yet kept on entering. Everywhere she goes, something goes wrong. People she meets end up dead. She was in a lot of foster homes and adopted by the hotel owners at a young age. She has a scar on her face and scars all over her body which she hides very well. These were from anger tantrums she had as a child and never grew out of even in adulthood. She had cut herself multiple times as a child in anger. She had a rage everyone knew of yet her parents kept her faults hidden like all of her dark secrets. I was called on by her parents multiple times to help her and talk with her yet she would never come into my church, or any other place of worship."

He had a glass of water and then said, "As a preacher, I meet troubled children and adults all the time. I tried to help all the children I could. At first, it never bothered me that Aideen Bakker was so strange. I assumed it was due to her various foster parents. I presumed as a grown-up woman, she had changed, and it was she who had employed my daughter. She had said it was her soft side that honestly wanted to help a preacher's daughter in need. Aideen cried a lot after my daughter's death and left the country and has not come back in three years. I should have followed my original feelings and known if she was so evil, she would be an expert at pretending to be nice. She was all fake and nothing in her was real."

He sat down as he was trembling in anger and said, "My child had lived in that hotel and helped them run the place twenty-four hours a day. She was murdered there by that woman and I know you will figure out why very soon. Yet how did she do it, for that detail, you will need the helping hands of the doctor who had fought to save her all these years and also had examined her after the incident. I believe Dr. Jacobus is the only one who can help."

I asked him, "Why do you think my brother can solve the mystery if we don't know anything about it yet?"

He watched outside toward the graveyard as the rain poured nonstop outside. I thought he was trying to think how much he could share.

Deep in his own thoughts he then said, "If you all can figure out why she did it, then I know he can help you solve the case. He is coming back from Tennessee, where he was involved in a case study which he believes will help. He said he can't share anything else as it's a very top-secret project. He did not even share with his family. Yet if that evil woman is the she-devil herself, then I believe Dr. Jacobus is the good we need in humanity himself. I believe the good spirits of Kasteel Vrederic will always guide you and your family members."

I knew I was supposed to have spent my summer with my big brother and parents in Tennessee but I switched places with my friend so Mama and Papa too stayed here. I also knew Jacobus was involved in a top-secret project as he was helping someone or something and that's how Papa and I got involved in this case. He asked us to do a favor. I thought the Kasteel Vrederic spirits must have somehow been involved as they did send the fortune teller. Yet I knew my family and my big brother so we never pushed for answers. For Big Papa always said, the answers are found only with time.

I asked the preacher, "I understand everything my brother is doing, for he is trying to help the government solve the mysterious deaths that link one with another through the same artist globally and in the same countries where the Mirrorless Hotel exists. Somehow linked are the woman and the hotel and the murders to one another. Yet why could the international investigators not be able to solve this case? What puzzles me more is how much more proof are they waiting for?"

The preacher said, "Your brother through his magical medical hands will solve the case, I am positive. Also you will through your ability to see in the dark. A painter who paints in the dark can catch a painter who is the dark. I pray someone comes back from the dead and testifies against the she-devil."

Big Mama whispered to herself loudly, "If only the dead could come back, I would do anything to get back my son right now, yet I know he will be back somehow."

The preacher heard her as we all did and he replied, "Miracles do happen. Your son will be back, maybe even now he is trying to come back. Be patient and all shall be."

Big Mama said, "I am a mother. I don't want to be patient. Erasmus, I really don't want to be patient."

She was crying silently again. Big Papa got up, held on to her, and said, "Baby, you are my strength and glowing hope. Be strong for our boys and me."

They held on to one another as I went, hugged my mother, and got her a glass of water. She kissed me and relaxed.

Big Papa then got up and looked outside through the same window that oversaw the graveyard and asked, "How did you know we would need your help to get out? Why were you there at the time of our need?"

The preacher watched me for a while and said, "Jacobus called me after he tried to reach all of you. He said one of his patients told him. As the patient had awakened from her sleep, she said she had a dream his parents are in danger. He called me and asked me to keep an eye on all of you as he said the dreamer was very clear as to the directions. The hotel wall that faces the graveyard side had a trap door and you three would come out from that side. The patient is a dreamer and has premonitions in dreams. As I understand, Dr. Jacobus himself believes in dreams. He said the only woman he has given his complete heart to, his mother, too is a dreamer."

We stayed at his place through the night and went over the mysterious chest we had not forgotten to bring with us amidst the looming dangers of being caught. I sought some magical help from the mysterious box. I opened the box and saw there were a lot of receipts in it. An album with photo negatives said, "Mirrorless Hotel Global." Then, there was another negative which was labeled, "World's Most Beautiful Woman In The Mirror."

I knew these negatives were our proof of the victims and their predator. All night, Big Papa and I went through each negative as Big Mama stayed awake talking about how Big Papa and Big Mama met and finally united, with the preacher. I watched Big Papa smile now and then as he too recollected his thoughts, he just enjoyed watching my mother his twin flame with the love of a "forever be mine."

After the dark night had passed, we had all the proof we needed and why, with us. They were the most gruesome murders that might be recorded in history. A very unhealthy, mentally unstable woman had kept a diary with her negatives that did not need any labels. I developed the pictures one by one and saw the portraits of the victims in real photographs, catching the last breath of each victim. Each woman had a title she had won in a local portrait competition. Not a beauty contest but each person's pictures were entered to win a portrait competition that actually was locally held around the globe.

The irony was that Aideen too had entered all of these local competitions. Some competitions were held locally, so they did not even make the newspapers. Some were held within family and friends and not even reported in any newspaper to even be traceable. Yet all of them had one connection, Aideen too had entered yet never won.

I said out loud, "It seems Miss Aideen Bakker, you are always the bridesmaid yet never the bride. For all the winners would get a portrait of themselves hung in their local museum as the most beautiful women. Yet Aideen had a replica portrait of herself made as the winner with the real winner's body and her face forged into it as the winner."

We found out there were notes on the negatives that had Aideen's name on different portraits of different women's faces. It was so strange as if the woman was psychotic. Why she would have her face on other people's bodies, we could not understand.

That's when the door opened as a new face we were not familiar with walked into the small kitchen of the preacher's cottage. He was about six feet, six inches tall and had blond hair and gray-blue eyes. He was very fit and had a beard like his friend. Big Mama with her Indian side went along and made fresh coffee for everyone. She also made vegetarian omelets and toast. All of this she did by digging into the preacher's small fridge without asking. He too watched her in amusement and just nodded at Big Papa and said nothing.

The new guest was asked to join us by my mother. I had asked my mother at a very young age, what if we get one hundred people during lunch? What would you do? She had replied that's nonsense. How would so many people come uninvited? Yet if even twenty people do come, we will divide our food amongst twenty people. Actually, I had found out my mother's Indian and American grandmothers both like to always cook extra so if an unexpected guest does show up, we have more than enough to share.

My mother asked the gentleman who was obviously friends with the preacher, "If you don't mind, who are you? And why are you here this early in the morning?"

He smiled at her and said, "The toast and omelet are out of this world. Thank you for the breakfast, I did not even realize I was so hungry. I am Egisrico Beekhof, the groundskeeper of this church. I have taken care of this church and its grounds for the last forty years. I am here to help all of you with your search and maybe I would get to see Dr. Jacobus Vrederic van Philip and his brother the blind painter Antonius van Phillip as I am their big fan. I loved Andries van Phillip. I am his biggest fan. I wrote to him always and he had been so kind and answered all of my questions. I have all of his CDs signed by him. I loved his piano tours. I never missed a single show. His death left me broken into pieces."

I knew Big Mama would start to cry now as our pianist learned to play for her. He would play for her and me as he told me always he was my sight. My mother had said on every note of his piano, she could hear her heartbeats. Yet our mother had stopped listening to pianos ever since Andries had passed away. Big Papa interrupted the conversation as he kissed Big Mama and just held on to her without saying anything.

Big Mama said, "You all just watch and see my son is coming back soon. He just needed a change, that's all."

Big Papa sat down and started to drink his morning coffee as he said, "How can you help us in this situation and how can you guide us toward a direction? I believe we know who did it. We are quite positive we know why it was done. Yet would you be able to tell us anything to help prove this theory as a fact?"

The graveyard and church groundskeeper Egisrico from Dokkum, Friesland said, "I am a firsthand witness to the murder. I was the person who had dug out the wounded woman in the middle of the night after I saw her being buried in the garden of the graveyard by a woman who wore a black cloak. I called the police and I called Jacobus as he always treats me and my family for free. I got free piano lessons for my kids from Andries too. I shall always be indebted to this kind family, eternally. I knew if anyone could help, it would be my Jacobus. Yet in the middle of the night, little did I know the woman was my best buddy's own daughter."

Egisrico started to cry out loud and I knew he was still in pain from the brutal night. We all just sat there watching nothing but being oblivious to everything quietly.

I got up and asked him, "It was dark. How do you know it was a woman who buried her?"

He watched me and said, "You should know how. I smelled her perfume. I listened to her breathing. I heard her footsteps, the footsteps of a fashionable woman always in heels. I knew the woman very well as I had worked for that hotel for ten years. I knew her evil ways, her anger, her rage, and her jealousy. She would come out and kill all the plants with her heels in anger. The parents could not say anything as always she would blackmail them and say they were mistreating her because she was adopted, not biological."

We all watched him as he continued, "I watched her bury the woman and say, 'You are so beautiful, you had to be dead. No one is more beautiful than me. You see you are not even a virgin. I made the guys rape you like an animal. No one would desire you anymore. I never kill anyone with my own hands as there are so many needy people in this world who need financial help like you.' She was laughing and jumping up and down as she said, 'Now since you are dead, in this area I am the most beautiful virgin woman available.' She was mad I tell you! Mad like Hell! I then made a sound like the nightingales of the night and started to sing, 'Aideen you are beautiful.' She said, 'I know little birdie, I am.' To answer your question Antonius, that's how I knew. I tested her out. The only way she broke out of pretense was when a bird too told her she is beautiful. She is so crazy, I am telling you, she never questioned how a little bird knew her name."

He watched his friend Ghileyn and knew it was too much for him. Yet I watched the two men and I saw the preacher just nodded his head and gestured to continue.

Egisrico then watched out of the window toward the graveyard as he said, "I called Jacobus first even though I knew he was not reachable for personal reasons. I then called the cops and told them what I saw and they arrested me for the crime. I had my best friend with me who knew I was telling the complete truth. He too was with me in the police station. Luckily the time of death or rape gave me freedom, but placed no one under suspicion. As I told the cops who I saw commit the crime, Aideen said she was not even in the country at the time. She said she was in Brussels and came in late. Her parents testified she was in Brussels as did two other men whom I never saw in my life."

He helped himself to a glass of water and gave his friend a glass. It was then the preacher had spoken after listening to everyone for so long.

Preacher Ghileyn said, "I believed Egisrico because I was his witness. He was here in my cottage watching the news on the television set. His favorite pianist Andries van Phillip had just passed away in a tragic car accident. He was crying and broken down into pieces as he saw something outside. When he went outside, I too watched the whole incident from within my home. Yet I was praying for another man, Andries's twin brother, who was fighting for his life. I never met him but wanted to meet him at least once in my lifetime. As a caretaker of the graveyard, Egisrico usually has young men he has to take care of for they come in and get drunk or hide for unknown reasons. I knew Andries and his brother Dr. Jacobus who is my doctor to go to for any advice. He never charges and gives everyone in this church free services."

Then he kept silent for a while and said, "When Jacobus finally did receive my daughter's dead body, I had not been able to say anything as I too knew what he was going through."

The whole room went into silence as if nothing more could be said. I knew the pain my brother was going through that night. He lost one brother and tried his best to save yet another brother. I could not think of anything as at that moment, my heartbeats just wanted to hear my brother's heartbeat one more time.

I could still hear our Big Mama's screams from that horrific night when I woke up from my own surgery performed by my brother Jacobus. The silent night too ripped through the air as she cried and screamed through the night.

Big Mama kept on saying, "How could your heart not beat if your heart beats Big Mama, and Big Mama's heart beats my three sons?"

I had only asked everyone, "What did my brother say that night, as I was not there to help him. Instead of being a shoulder for him to lean on, I laid in the hospital bed letting him take upon his shoulders all the heavy weight."

Preacher Ghileyn continued, "Jacobus spoke to the police who were brutally mean with him as they kept on asking him for answers as to how she died. When was she raped? Was there any proof from the rape that would help them? Jacobus was a little late and they all told him a doctor can never be late."

He watched Big Mama and said, "Jacobus apologized to the police and told them, 'I had a very dear guest who had entered my life at a very young age. Today I had to bid my farewell to the same guest.' I watched him and knew he was talking about his brother and all of my pain disappeared as I hugged him and prayed with him. I knew whatever happened to my child was my fate, yet I will find out who had done it and how. I wanted to be there for Jacobus at the time when he was the shoulders for his parents and all of his patients without even wanting a shoulder to lean on."

He walked around and said, "I also told Jacobus to find out if there was any link with my daughter's death and his brother's car accident. On that day, I had heard Aideen tried to get a signed copy of Andries's CD. She was flirting with him while he was here trying to see Egisrico. She said how dare a famous sexy man avoids her and comes and visits a low-life church caretaker. She said she would not forget his insults. Andries only laughed and said he has seen ugly in his life but she was capital ugly in person. He also said if his Big Mama saw her, she would slap her until she couldn't slap anymore."

I told everyone, "I know who has committed the crime as I saw the dark lab where she had stored all the proof. Her dark signature was left with her victims. She can't even paint, so she forged her talent. Through a computer program, she forged the pictures to appear as portraits. She even fooled museums yet I could tell just by touching the portraits with my hands. My sixth sense gave me an advantage which a normal painter might see or miss. Yet I wonder if she did have something to do with the car accident because we were really close by and how our car happened to be where it was could never be explained."

I thought to myself why I could not remember that night, as if it was erased from my memories. I knew Big Mama watched me as she came and held on to me.

She said, "If that woman is a snake, I am still a mother and I will find out what happened by bringing my child back from the dead."

I told everyone, "The predator is a forger, not a painter as she has declared the paintings to be of a famous artist, known as unknown. She is the counterfeit dark painter who takes pictures of her victims' crime scenes and forges them as oil paintings she had created, for immoral pleasures.

I will fight for all my fellow artists for this forger has tainted our reputation. I am an artist, a painter, who shall take this as a challenge and catch her in her own games, for she lives in the dark and I paint in the dark. Also if she is involved in any way in the murder of my brother, I will take my revenge in my own time. My oath from above and the beyond is I shall unravel the murder mystery."

Dear beloved, please know I shall solve this mystery and unite with you either on Earth or Heaven above for where there is love, there are no worries about waiting for one another as you are eternally mine. This is my eighth poem written simply for you.

UNRAVEL THE MURDER MYSTERY

For you my beloved,
I live my life for I know
You have so bravely crossed over
And come back through my dreams.

You guide me through love.

You give me strength

Through your courage.

Your determination

Becomes my living will.

This world was and still is a challenge

For me to survive through,

Yet I have taken

The vows of a beloved.

With all my living heartbeats,

I shall avenge

For your short-lived life,

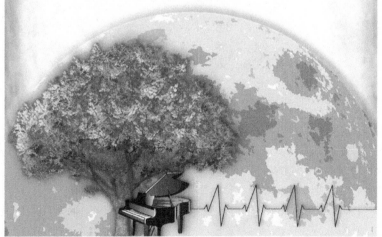

As my vows

Shall guide me,

For I shall

With all my love,

UNRAVEL THE MURDER MYSTERY.

Signed: Antonius van Phillip

CHAPTER EIGHT:

The Walking Dead Woman

"Pronounced dead by the world means they are no more, yet even beyond death, they can still see us and feel for us, so how are they no more? For what happens when the dead come back and ask but I saw you and felt for you, how could you not see me or feel me, yet call me the walking dead woman?"

Jacobus Vrederic van Phillip enters with a huge surprise and as always is the biggest shoulders of support for his family.

The Mirrorless Hotel had seen its better days. Today the owners were trying to figure out a way to get customers back into their haunted hotel. Rumors of their daughter and her lifestyle came into question by others aside from my family members. When we walked into the hotel lobby, we were greeted with emotionless vibes of the empty hotel.

I tried to figure out what was going in the minds of parents who actually thought their child might be involved in murder. My eyes followed them yet my sixth sense followed a certain sound of heartbeats. Again I saw the grand piano in the lobby started to play on its own. The musical notes were very familiar as Andries, the pianist, was also the composer of this musical classic.

This was one of his famous compositions. I tried to see who was playing the piano yet saw no one. Then I saw on the piano was a small child whom I could see through. He became even more transparent, yet his hands were so talented and magical. My family tried to see where the music was coming from yet no one else paid any heed to it. I watched Big Mama and Big Papa sitting and talking with the preacher Ghileyn and the caretaker Egisrico in the hotel café as they all sat there and were enjoying a meal together.

The hotel's restaurant guests were making a crowd near Big Papa to get a picture with him. I watched Big Mama smile and enjoy the crowd unlike normal wives. She is a one-of-a-kind woman, whom I know Big Papa loves more than he loves to breathe. He watches her all the time, even when he is talking to others. I know they want to make up for the years they had searched for one another and missed out being together.

Then Livina said, "I heard you all are leaving us tomorrow. So this will be your last night here. I wonder were you able to tell anything or gather any clues from inspecting all the portraits? It's absolutely normal as after three years, I would think the police would have found something if there was anything. They told us it was a cold case. What is your opinion?"

I was shocked at her questions, for I knew she was so nervous and tried to find out if we knew anything or if we were getting closer to their daughter. I only smiled and signed some papers.

I told her, "It was a nice stay yet we miss our home. We live close by and can return if we need anything. We will keep our room for a few more days, so if we need anything, we can return. We will not be staying here but will still pay for the family suite."

I avoided answering her questions and wondered would she pry more for the answers or just pretend she never even asked? I somehow thought I heard heartbeats and I watched Big Mama look in the direction I too was watching. There the young child stood alone waiting for someone.

I watched him come and sit closer to Big Papa as I watched Big Papa move aside giving him space to sit. Big Mama and Big Papa both watched one another yet said nothing. I wondered then was the boy traveling with my parents or my mystical princess? For today I did not see my princess but just the child.

I pondered, could spirits leave their children in the care of others? Did she leave him with my parents? But why? And where was she? It was then I saw a woman enter the café area of the hotel. She was all full of richness and arrogance. She came in and screamed at the cleaning crew. I saw Livina's hands had started to shake more than normal. She was terrified in fear as if she saw a ghost. I realized the cold vibes of the day came from this new visitor who walked with so much terror. I walked blindly so I was used to not seeing any terror even if it walked in front of me.

Livina said very quietly only for my ears, "That's Aideen. Please be careful. For if she is my daughter, then I consider you my son and Katelijne Snaaijer my other daughter whom I could not protect. With God as my witness, I will take her down myself if I could prove my inner feelings. I know she is hiding something and now I fear for my life and of my husband's. I wish you all could stay a while more until she is gone for my own safety."

It was then I realized the complete truth of a mother's dilemma. She loved her daughter yet knew in her mind, this was an evil child she could not protect herself from or protect all others from. The woman walked closer toward Big Papa as I walked closer to my parents and put my glasses on. Before I left, I asked Livina, "Please do not let anyone know about my sight."

The woman only nodded as I walked away. I went and used my cane to find my mother. I realized my parents immediately knew what I was up to and played along. The woman went closer to my father and was watching him like a sick puppy.

She said, "Erasmus van Phillip in my hotel. I must have done something good today. Or is it you too find me irresistible like I find you sweetheart?"

Big Papa stood up and said, "The only person I find attractive is my enchantingly beautiful wife. She has mesmerized me throughout time. Not even death could separate us from one another."

The woman actually glanced at my very petite mother up and down and smirked.

Big Mama never keeps her feelings hidden as she said, "You seem to be a desperate virgin who lacks all basic moral values, and have no shame talking to married men. Why don't you find yourself a man and spread your legs and just get it over with? Since you have no moral values, may I ask you what is keeping you single, when it's so obvious you don't want to be? Or is it that you offer everything for free, and even then no one finds you interesting?"

The woman was so angry she was jumping up and down as Big Mama said, "Don't jump like a frog or you will get stomped over by who knows who, maybe by a small petite person like myself. In anger, you will trip over yourself and then everyone will really see you are dirty and ugly, inside and outside. As a mother, I suggest you should go and get a clean shower for you smell like a dirty load of laundry."

The woman said very calmly, "I like you. I am Aideen Bakker, the owner of this hotel. If you do need anything, don't forget to ask me personally. I will make sure your stay is as comfortable as possible."

Big Mama smiled and said, "I am your guest who actually pays for your lifestyle. I don't need anything, but I warn you, do not take away what you can never give back to me or anyone else. Also, I don't think you can actually help me for you don't have anything left to give anyone anyway."

I watched the furious woman was about six feet, four inches tall with dirty blonde hair and deep blue eyes. I realized she could have easily been Miss Universe yet her inside made her into Miss Devil herself. She walked and talked with anger and arrogance. Even an unknown person could see through her eyes and know she was full of disgrace. She almost bumped into me as I did not budge. I knew she was trying to see if I could see or not as the miracle behind my sight was not known to all as of yet.

Aideen said, "I am sorry, I had assumed you were able to see, yet I believe you still can't see. You are missing out on seeing how amazingly handsome you are. I would love to be able to get to know you more closely. Actually, I am a painter too. I love your paintings and have admired your whole family excluding your mother."

I knew it was her slip of a tongue as she never publicly announced herself as the painter behind the murdered victims. She had said she does not paint publicly.

I told her, "I am blind in sight not in knowledge. I can see you are ugly as anyone who is not a fan of my beautiful mother is not my friend but an outright enemy. I did not know a hotel owner too paints, for I never knew the only heiress of the Mirrorless Hotel is an artist. For some reason your smell is very familiar, as if we had met somewhere, sometime. I will remember with time."

She knew she made a huge mistake, so she tried to cover herself up and said, "Hey guys I am just kidding. I can't paint and I am a fan of Anadhi as I did read your amazing books. I hope my jokes did not come out wrong."

I told her, "I don't see wrong or right. Actually, I can't see anything but I can feel everything. I was not joking about your smell. I am positive I had encountered you as I don't forget my smells."

I saw Big Papa come and stand next to me and said, "We will be leaving soon so we won't be in your way, as we were your only living guests aside from your restaurant guests. Now you will have all the time to do some renovation which I hear your mother has planned for a while."

Aideen then said, "No we have guests. Did you not hear the pianist playing the piano? He was just playing over there."

It was then Livina came over and said, "Sweetheart, our hotel is haunted and this kind family was here trying to help and guide us. Somehow the police think it's the murdered women, whose bodies they had recovered over the years, have all returned. No one wants to believe it but actually the piano has been playing, and the windows and doors open and close. We also hear cries and screams of women rip off throughout the nights. Also the piano keeps playing Andries van Phillip's compositions, his famous musical notes, all day and all night."

I knew the piano was playing on its own but what was Livina saying? I watched her as she was looking into my eyes to convey a message I played along with, even though I did not know what was going on.

Livina continued to talk, "This kind family has only come to help us and find the real criminal who has done all of this. Your father has taken ill and is in need of hospitalization. So even Dr. Jacobus Vrederic van Phillip is coming over to check on him and then he will take his family home with him. He just gave me a call and we were on the phone trying to figure out your father's situation. Also the police are trying to investigate why the piano keeps on playing Andries's compositions."

I realized Jacobus had planned this in advance to his arrival. I wondered what Jacobus was planning. I only saw an angry woman stomp her high heels and scream for nothing. Also why was everyone talking about Andries now? Did this woman have anything to do with our car accident that night? How did Andries and I end up at the bottom of the hill and go over a curve? Why can't I remember?

She said to her mother, "I saw Dad this morning after I arrived. He was fine. What are you saying now? Why did you not say anything before? What ghosts and why are you bringing in people to my hotel when I never needed any help? I want everyone out of my hotel. There are no ghosts and I don't believe in any ghosts. Also if there is a ghost, we can easily get rid of it too. I don't think any pianist that had died by sliding his car off a hill and hitting the curve is haunting us anyway."

We all looked up and wondered how she knew how Andries had died. We had never reported the details surrounding the accident, but only that he had passed away in a tragic car accident. Big Papa warned all of us not to say anything through his eyes. We all knew she just might have incriminated herself by slipping information no one except our family knew.

Big Mama changed the subject as she came closer to me and whispered loudly, "I wonder why tall women wear heels. They are tall anyway!"

Amongst all of this, Aideen said, "It makes us feel sexy, and what kind of a question is that?"

Big Mama continued, "Obviously you are in pain from lifting heavy things as your feet are suffering from it. I wonder how you managed to wear heels even though you are suffering from it. Are you used to getting your ways even though it hurts you and others? Also you keep on saying you are the owner of the hotel, yet to my knowledge, your parents are the owners. How will you get rid of ghosts? You get rid of anyone who does not suit you. Who else did you get rid of that irritated you too?"

The angry woman said nothing as she stomped away to her mother. I watched Big Mama as I had nothing to say over my mother. Big Papa only kissed her and hugged her in his arms. I wondered what was going on in my mother's head as I knew she is a psychic and knew she was up to something. It was then I watched Big Mama and saw she was watching something in front of her. I followed her gaze and saw the child show something.

I watched the door and saw my mother jump up. Her emotions betrayed her as there was only one person on Earth who could do that. I knew my big brother must be standing behind me. The wind blew in the air as a cold and warm feeling had filled the room. I heard musical notes rip the Earth from a mystical land. The lights flickered as the daytime storm had converted a nice summer day into a dark cloudy day. We needed the lights to be turned on.

My big brother Jacobus walked in through the front door. He looks so much like Big Papa yet he is six feet tall with brown hair and brown eyes. He has an amazing French beard which makes him look identical to the diarist Jacobus van Vrederic. He came in front of Big Mama and gave her a huge hug as he lifted her in his arms and twirled with her and kissed her on her two cheeks.

He then said, "Mama's heart beats Jacobus."

I watched my Big Mama cry and say nothing for the only time in her life she can never say anything was when my big brother Jacobus hugs or kisses her. Jacobus went to Big Papa and gave him a hug.

He said, "Love you Papa. I hope you are able to keep Mama off her feet. Yet I miss my great-grandmothers and especially Nani's home-cooked meals. Let's go home everyone."

I hugged my brother as I knew it was very emotional as we both missed Andries, yet somehow I kept on hearing a certain heartbeat that kept on ringing in my ears. I watched my big brother look in the direction of the spirit child and smiled in acknowledgement. It was then I saw Jacobus watch in a certain direction and smile without saying anything.

He then said silently only to our ears, "I would like to introduce you to one of my patients. She was in my care for the last three years. She laid in a complete coma for the last three years. I had treated her and can finally say she is a complete success. I had become like her big brother through the years. I will give you all the complete details as we go home. But she wanted to be here in this hotel first before she begins her new life. All of you just play along with us and don't acknowledge her physically. The boy you see is a spirit who will be born from within the walls of Kasteel Vrederic. I promise it is then Mama will be complete with her three sons."

I watched in the direction he was staring at and saw a woman walk in through the door. A woman, five feet, eight inches tall, with brown hair and brown eyes. Olive-colored skin proving she is mixed race, maybe Italian and Dutch origin. Dressed in a white summer dress, she walked in like a blessed ray of the morning sun. The pouring rain outside had stopped. The dark day became a nice summer day. The only proof there even was a storm was left in our memories.

I watched a dead woman walk not in the form of a ghost but a human with grace and dignity. She immediately saw the spirit child as she looked in that direction. I saw the spirit boy go and hold her hands. I didn't know if she saw him or not, but he knew this was his mother just as my inner soul knew they are my family.

We all pretended to not see the woman as she went straight to the piano and started to play notes composed and played by my brother Andries. She was so graceful, yet somehow I knew she kept looking at me as I too wondered how the woman who had flooded my dreams for the last three years was in front of me. The same woman who was brutally murdered here at this hotel, and the same woman who had been living here like a ghost spirit for the last three years. I saw behind Jacobus were clearly standing the spirits of Kasteel Vrederic.

Preacher Ghileyn and his friend Egisrico showed no reaction. I realized how hard it must be for a father to see his child and not say anything yet he did just that. The hotel owner Livina came over as she began to tremble. She hugged Jacobus as he too hugged her back.

He said, "Livina, it's so nice to see you again. I hope you are taking care of your handsome husband. He is getting old and needs to keep up with his health. Otherwise, it will be too late to do anything. I must ask him again to get admitted to the hospital and get his heart surgery done."

She was shaking and said, "I will make him get admitted. I don't want to risk his life for anything. Jacobus, who is that woman who walked with you?"

Jacobus laughed and said, "Sweetheart, if there was a woman walking with me, my mother would have known. It would either be a friend, girlfriend, or a sister. I don't have any of the above. Anyway, my mother would have known before I even go out and date. We were asked by our mother to date or get a girlfriend with her blessings only."

It was then Jacobus left to check on Luyt to prepare him for an open-heart surgery. I realized Jacobus always pays a home visit to patients he knows need a surgery on an emergency basis.

I saw the self-proclaimed hotel owner, Aideen, return. She was trying to see what was still happening in the lobby. Yet my parents had left to be in our room. Jacobus was with the owners. I waited with a drink in my hands as I knew the person who called me with her heartbeats was still playing the piano. The preacher and his friend too had left for the day.

The amazing beauty had her back toward the receptionist's front desk. The astonishing gorgeousness was gracefully playing the piano. I watched Aideen walk toward her and tried to grab her attention. Aideen tried to call a few times yet as our guest never answered, the host went a little crazy. I knew Aideen had a raging temper and I wanted to see when she would go out of control. Jacobus had returned and stood behind at the corner watching everything.

Aideen then said, "Excuse me, I am happy you are enjoying our piano, but we are not taking any new customers into our hotel for a few days due to some renovation projects. You could, however, enjoy the food in our unique and quiet reputable restaurant café."

She waited for a while as our pianist seemed busy playing the piano only. It was after Aideen kept on screaming for a while our pianist stood up now facing Aideen completely. I watched my beautiful mystical princess watch her predator straight in the eyes.

Aideen screamed like she just saw a ghost. Then she walked backward trying to see with her eyes the new arriving guest of the hotel. I watched the little spirit boy return and start to play the piano. He kept on playing while the mystical princess kept on watching Aideen. Then I saw and heard for the first time in reality not in my dreams, the musical sweet voice of my mystical princess.

She said, "I, Katelijne Snaaijer, am back. Like the blinking stars of Heaven, I am going to blink all over this hotel. I traveled to and back from Heaven to let this world know who you are. Also I do wonder, did you unveil all of the mirrors in your private chamber? They say the same thing. You are ugly from inside out. You can't murder all of the women you feel threatened by because you are so ugly. Go disrobe the mirrors. They will show you, how truly ugly you are. You can't put away all the mirrors in this world you know."

I wanted to burst out into laughter as I saw Katelijne stop and gather her thoughts. I realized how much she was like Big Mama and did not fear the predators or shy away from any threat but was brave and a true warrior who would fight for the innocent. I understood she was the victim who had come back to face her brutal predator without fear.

Katelijne continued, "No one finds you beautiful because you see your true self in the mirror. Did you know what you see in the mirror is what everyone sees of you in reality, a murderer? Your true reflection shows in all of your hidden mirrors. You had killed me mercilessly as you had your goons rape and brutally injure me and throw me into the graveyard, where you buried me alive."

I had closed my eyes in pain of thinking what she had gone through. Yet I watched her watch me for any acknowledgement. I hope she did not misunderstand me because there was nothing in this world that would make her any less attractive to me. I watched her nod and knew she could read my mind. I knew Big Mama had said twin flames can read minds.

I told her mind to mind, "If you can hear me, please nod or say yes."

She then did nod and said, "Yes I can."

The raging woman was still huffing and puffing in the lobby. She screamed and shrieked, "I don't believe you can do anything as you are dead or if you are here, then you're not the same person for I know I had killed and buried you alive. Ha-ha, pretty face, you can never prove anything to anyone because you are dead and I am still alive."

I had all of her words on tape as I carried my cell phone for that reason. She then ran toward the cellar where I knew the police were waiting for her. My parents came into the lobby as did the preacher and his friend who had been the only suspect of the police. No one had believed a father and his words as everyone dismissed his words saying he was only the stepfather.

Yet Jacobus never gave them a deaf ear as he had healed with his blessed hands the woman presumed dead. I watched our Kasteel Vrederic spirits walk with Jacobus and knew they were always with him, guiding him. Big Mama came with Jacobus as did the hotel owners.

Luyt then asked Jacobus, "Will you now at least tell everyone how everything actually happened? And when did you find out who the criminal is? We the parents did not know anything until you called us for help. Like I told you, I will never protect a criminal, family or not. Still, I really need to know where we went wrong."

I watched my brother as he only smiled and said, "First things first, you need to get admitted into that hospital now. You did nothing wrong as a parent. A parent only raises a child to be an adult. An adult then takes and makes his or her own decisions. My Mama has told me, she taught me to drive a car so I can handle this huge machine carefully. How I handle it is my choice. My mother also said, she herself is scared to drive on a road. There are so many wild and crazy drivers, so she has hired a permanent driver for life, my Papa."

We all went downstairs and saw the police say Aideen had run away through a tunnel she had built years ago. She left a note for me as it read,

Dear Antonius van Phillip,

Congratulations you have figured out how I murdered all of those women throughout the years. I *only wish you could have figured it out earlier as then not only would Dr. Jacobus Vrederic van Phillip's pretend ghost be alive but your twin brother too.*

I guess you will never know now what happened to your twin brother. I killed him because he wanted to be a brave warrior and save a damsel in distress, so he is dead. Yet none of you will ever find me to prove this. See you, maybe on the other side.

Signed,

Delicious tempting mirror on the wall,
Who watches over for me above all,
As he knows I, Aideen, am the most temptingly
Beautiful woman in this world.

Everyone read the letter that was taken away as evidence by the police. It never bothered me that the woman ran away for I knew we would find her. Yet I wondered what she meant about my brother Andries. We all watched Big Mama as she was crying and trying to be brave at the same time.

She watched the woman who stood in the room as she had in her hands a tiny little see-through hand, everyone in our family could see but no one said anything.

Big Mama said, "Erasmus take our sons and me home please. I want to take all of them back home with me."

Big Mama then said, "Katelijne Snaaijer, please come home with us as you have someone with you who belongs to our family. Please don't deny my wish as I must take all of them back home to Kasteel Vrederic, for the spirits of Kasteel Vrederic to help."

Silence gripped all around the hotel as I thought no birds could even be heard for there were tears from heart-gripping pain. Waterfalls erupted from a crying mother who once again lost her son. A mother today again found out her son might have died because of premeditated murder, not a plain car accident. I watched a small young baby boy who held on to the hands of his mother. He kept on looking at Big Mama.

As a spirit, I knew he could only watch yet not comfort maybe an unknown woman. I wondered whether children feel other people's pain more than adults ever could. I knew again I must wait out with the wagon of time for the answers. Now we had with us someone who too was amongst the dead but was now our glowing hope as she was the walking dead woman.

My ninth poem is written only for you my beloved for one day I will give my love poems that are also my vows for you, to only you.

THE WALKING DEAD WOMAN

From death, my love, you have risen.
Today you are walking again
Amongst the living
Yet with dignity, honor, and courage.
My heartbeats had called your name
As I had listened
To your gifted heartbeats,

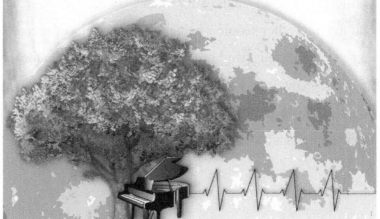

Which were played within my ears,

By a little pianist.

My blind eyes found you in my dreams,

As my sight found you

Within my inner soul

For even when nothing was known,

Even then within my dreams,

I found you.

Gracefully, you entered

My awakening life

Yet I only wish

You remember me,

From the dreamy nights we shared,

And the magical nights we treasured.

May these sweet memories not end.

Remember me,

Oh my beloved living,

THE WALKING DEAD WOMAN.

Signed: Antonius van Phillip

CHAPTER NINE:

Remember Me Eternally

"The buried walls of a castle can't speak or share all the stories hidden within its walls. For if only it could share and tell, then we could hear them and gain knowledge from the past and move with it to the future. All the lost stories would then be found and the only portraits left on the walls would be 'remember me eternally.'"

The van Phillip family members enter their home Kasteel Vrederic and gather in front of the Lover's Lighthouse.

T he door of death was never feared in this home we call Kasteel Vrederic. Our historians have gone back through time through the blessed pages of our ancestor Jacobus van Vrederic who had brought back his only daughter in a coffin to this home. It made him suffer more than he thought was even possible. Yet through his journey, he had found the blessed heartbeats of his life, the loving granddaughter of Kasteel Vrederic, Margriete "Rietje" Jacobus Peters, from whose lineage the family tree continued.

Today we came home without a son, a brother, and a grandson who was lost through murder, revenge, and rage of an unjust woman who only lived to hate. I knew Jacobus and I would not rest until we found the answers and got the culprit. Yet tonight we all wanted our mother to be back home within the walls of Kasteel Vrederic. For within these walls, Mama found answers to all her emotional burdens. We all entered the courtyard of Kasteel Vrederic where Big Mama almost collapsed in front of the Lover's Lighthouse.

Big Papa held on to her and did not allow anything to happen to Big Mama. Jacobus and I held on to Mama from two sides as we all just stood there under the starless cloudy night. I knew the Lover's Lighthouse shows the spirits of Kasteel Vrederic kissing when true lovers find one another or pray in front of the lighthouse. Yet for the first time we saw them in the Mirrorless Hotel. Maybe they wanted to bring a son of Kasteel Vrederic back home with them.

So I knew this was going to be a bitter night or just maybe we would be blessed by them again miraculously. Then I saw next to Jacobus came in Katelijne, who only gasped watching the glowing lighthouse. There inside of it was a kissing couple and I watched Katelijne as she watched me and had touched my shoulders. We both just watched one another and knew the lighthouse spirits had just blessed us.

Big Mama said in her crying voice, "One of my sons has found his twin flame. I am blessed as I know which one has and this is a blessing from the beyond. Yet dear spirits of Kasteel Vrederic who have promised to always show true lovers and true love, why then has a mother's prayers gone unseen? I wonder was there any deficiency in my motherly love? For I never differentiated amongst my boys. Tell me how could my heart beat when my son's heart beats no more?"

I watched Jacobus watch Big Mama for a while and say, "Mama, life is a strange journey where I believe you know I am the incarnation of Jacobus van Vrederic. It is strange yet I still remember the day I had brought my daughter Griet, the spirit of Kasteel Vrederic, home in a coffin while I watched my son-in-law whom I loved like a son walk into the coffin injured. I wanted to hold on to my child and even prayed if I could have held her at least once. I wanted to switch places with her on that day. I could not, but I got another gift, a gift I treasured then and we all treasure today, my granddaughter Rietje. I still hear her words, 'Opa's heart beats Rietje.' Today we are all here because of her. Have faith Mama. You too will get a blessed gift, for watch the lighthouse. What is happening in there?"

We all watched the Lover's Lighthouse and in there was the heartbeat symbol with a child's face glowing ever brightly. I realized why the spirits of Kasteel Vrederic had traveled tonight. They wanted to see a son come back home to his mother yet as a grandson. It was then I saw next to Katelijne stood a young baby boy, who was watching Big Mama and was crying.

The night did not seem to pass as my two great-grandmothers, whom we the boys call Nani and Grandmother, came outside. They were elderly and I knew age was taking a toll on them. Yet somehow both women kept each other strong and young. I watched them come and almost jump onto both of us.

Jacobus and I spoke in Dutch, Hindi, and English as taught by our mother from childhood. Suddenly Nani was watching Katelijne and tried to see something. I knew she was watching the young baby boy as she smiled and touched Katelijne.

She asked, "Do you speak Hindi? If not, then learn quickly."

Nani watched her for a while and said, "Look, you are so tall and I am a short woman. Bend your head so I can kiss you and bless you."

Katelijne laughed and smiled for the first time since I saw her. She then kissed my Nani and said, "I am tall so I can kiss you all the time, and here, now you can kiss me too."

Then she bent and gave both of my great-grandmothers a big hug. After everyone settled for the night, I found Jacobus in the courtyard sitting on stone paved ground next to Big Papa and Big Mama as he was massaging Big Mama's small feet. I sat next to him and started to massage Big Papa's feet. Our favorite time spent together as a family was sitting in our courtyard next to Mama and Papa and story time.

The only problem was Andries was missing. He had always stood behind Mama and Papa as he massaged their shoulders simultaneously. I then saw Katelijne walk into the courtyard. There again was the sound of heartbeats and a piano playing in the background. She just saw us and went and stood where Andries always stood and started to massage Mama and Papa just like he had done.

Jacobus smiled and just said, "Soon Mama, your son will be back. Yet I do have some things I must clear out before another dawn comes upon us. For I want the blessed dawn to come and bless our home."

Big Papa just watched Big Mama trying to see if she was ready for this. Big Mama also watched Big Papa and touched his hands with her own hands. I knew everything would be just all right.

Jacobus placed his head on Big Mama's lap as he said, "It started on the night of the accident. I had rushed to the hospital to find out not one but both of my brothers were involved in a tragic car accident. Antonius was badly injured and Andries was not. I tried to see the details of his injury when I realized his eyes were damaged. If only we could have had a complete eye transplant, then he would have a chance to ever see. For if we could not do it then, he would never have a chance of seeing. I was okay with that as long as my brother lived."

Jacobus never moved but continued, "It was then a cabin full of dead bodies was delivered to the same unit. All the women were brutally murdered and buried in different places. The hospital was full of parents and guardians of the newly found bodies. I tried to see Andries as he had awakened and wanted to talk with me."

Jacobus needed to take a breath as he stood up and watched the lighthouse glow in front of us. Yet he continued, "Andries told me he was poisoned by the daughter of a rich man. He does not know her, but a church preacher's daughter was brutally raped. He tried to save her. She was taken by a group of goons and he hid in the same van trying to save her. He said he was in the church praying with the church caretaker. He gave free piano lessons to him and his children. Some guys came and tied up the young woman and took her with them. The preacher was in a separate room praying while the caretaker was trying to make coffee for him. Andries ran after the van. After a very short ride, he said he watched the men rape her brutally and the evil woman had just sat there and had enjoyed her being raped. He fought to save the woman's honor yet the woman was knocked out through an injection."

Jacobus then started to make a fist and continued, "Andries tried to get himself and the woman out of there yet this evil woman had injected him with something and said Andries would soon taste the sweet aromas of death. He could not remember anything when he saw Antonius in his car. No one knows how Antonius appeared in his car, but I heard the same woman had drugged him and brought him there so both of them would die in a car accident and no one would ever know what Andries had seen."

I was trying to think what I could remember from that night. I told Jacobus, "I was going to finish up some work with Big Papa and Big Mama yet they went home. Andries had called and said he was going to see his friends, a preacher and the church caretaker, near Papa's art studio. So I waited for him to come over. I know someone came in. I know she was a female who used expensive perfumes. I didn't suspect anything but she helped me in her car and promised to take me to Andries. I tried to call Andries but he did not answer the phone. The next thing I knew, I was in the hospital and Jacobus was with me."

Jacobus then said, "So she had not planned for this, but Andries was at the wrong place at the wrong time. She was smart and tried to make it seem like an accident as she placed the car on drive and let it go at the top of the hill. Everyone assumed it was dark and Andries did not see the curve and fell to his death. He had awakened after the accident and had not even suffered a broken bone. He was, however, injected with a toxic poison of some kind that was purely sugar. He had type 1 diabetes and went into a shock. I realized the drug must have had some kind of sleeping aid and who knows what else was in it. We found the same injections were used on other victims. I think she used them before she had all the women raped, so it made them fall asleep immediately."

Jacobus got up as he checked his phone and continued without saying anything. None of us asked him who the caller was, for we knew he would share in his own time.

He then said, "The dead bodies kept on coming as I was busy with my brothers. I lost Andries and went into a shock myself. I just wanted to save the brother who was still breathing. In the emergency room, everything was dark. There were two bodies, my two brothers. One passed away and the other one was fighting for his life."

Big Papa got up and for the first time made a fist and said, "Continue son. I just wish you would have shared this with us before. It was too much to suffer by yourself. This Papa of yours is still breathing and would like my children to share their problems with me."

Jacobus then watched everyone and said, "I was bound by my medical oath and by the police not to share anything with anyone. It was a nightmare as in one room, I had dead bodies of young women, the police were waiting with. Yet I broke down and wept holding on to my two brothers. I know I should cry for all of the people brought into the hospital, yet this selfish brother wept for his two brothers and a mother whose crying screams broke the night. My mother's screams filled the air as she questioned the Lord for the first time in my life. She had asked if her love had anything lacking for she loved her three boys and wanted them home. I thought how could the Lord but keep quiet? It was then I saw in front of my eyes a miracle take place and knew the Lord did not keep quiet. Mama, he answered."

Big Mama got up and started to cry again as I watched Katelijne get up and hold Mama.

Katelijne then said, "It's all my fault. Nothing would have happened if I was just left alone with the murderer."

Jacobus then went to her and said, "Come on. You don't want all my hard work to go to waste. Let the tears roll out tonight but promise me no more tears after dawn. For after dawn, we shall rejoice new life and new beginnings."

I watched Katelijne nod in agreement. It was then Jacobus walked over to me and said, "So my brother, here is the rest of the story."

He then watched the stars and said, "Like a miracle from heavens above, I saw my dead brother rise into the air, and from his body, a child came out. The child came closer to me and had said, 'Uncle Jacobus help me. I need to be born. Actually that is my body, your brother's, and now I will be reborn as your nephew. Give my heartbeats a chance.' He then asked me to follow him as he took me to his earthly body and said, 'I gift my eyes to my brother and he will soon see me as his son.' He then took me to another room where all the dead bodies of the young women were kept. He showed me a body and told me, 'She is not dead as my heart beats her name.'"

Jacobus watched everyone and continued, "I saw then Antonius's spirit body was standing next to the same body. She then raised her hands and touched Antonius and said, 'Help me. I am your twin flame. Our child seeks us. Please help.'"

I got up and told everyone, "That was a dream I kept on having after my surgery. I had the nightmare over and over again. I even wanted to share with Jacobus but never did as I too did not want to burden everyone with all of my dreams or nightmares."

Jacobus then told us, "I did the two surgeries I never thought I would be able to complete as they were the first ones of their kind. My brother Andries's eyes gave sight to my brother Antonius which was the easier one amongst the two surgeries."

Jacobus glanced at Big Papa for a while. Big Papa gave him a nod of acknowledgement with his head.

Jacobus then said, "Andries also donated his heart to the woman he wanted to be born from and knew would be his mother. He kept on repeating he wanted to be Big Mama's child again. He wanted to be raised by only his Big Mama. The woman in particular was declared medically dead. Yet I had my feelings she was not dead, and I had to go against everyone to prove she was not dead. I had my brother Andries show me she was not dead, as I proved to the hospital she was still alive."

Jacobus watched Big Mama and she kissed his head as she held on to his hands.

Jacobus continued, "A complete heart surgery was never ever done on Earth. Katelijne's case was the first, yet with the help of the police department and some doctors from the Netherlands and then more doctors from the USA, it was a complete success. We were, however, told to keep this surgery a top secret as with the success, we would be able to catch the person or group responsible for a global murder mystery. More than two hundred women were killed yet there was no clue until Katelijne's case, as my two brothers interrupted a huge culprit from harming another innocent soul."

We all knew what happened after that as we all got involved and did what we could, yet without the details. It was strange how a single woman over twenty years had murdered so many women yet no one could link her to any one of these crimes. The police said they were all looking for a group of men raping and murdering these women. Yet I wondered what triggered the final clue.

Big Papa asked my thoughts out loud as he said, "The police had no clue for twenty years. Then how and from where did they get new clues suddenly?"

The police chief entered our home as he told Jacobus, "Dr. Jacobus, thank you for allowing us to come this late. We got your message and are happy to inform you we got the culprit. She was caught by her own parents. She was hiding in the cellar and had two of her famous injections ready to kill her parents with. She entered their bedroom as she had their nightly tea spiked with sleeping pills. Yet they were waiting for her. Two cops were hiding in their bedroom also. A fight broke out as she was ready with guns and injections. Yet Mrs. Livina Bakker-Beenhouwer shot her with the gun in front of the two police officers. It was sad as they said they had brought her into their home and gave her everything a parent could give, yet they had wronged in their upbringing and did not even realize they were raising a beast, not a human. They said it was a blessing as they were able to save two police officers whom the society need to protect all from evil women or men like Aideen."

There were four officers who had entered and I watched all of them had continuously watched the Lover's Lighthouse hoping for a miracle. But our spirits remained quiet as they too were overloaded with pain and grief.

The police chief told all, "The confession letter of the serial killer was all we needed as we had Dr. Jacobus's medical testimony as to how all the murders and even the poisoning was handled. Yet we just could not figure out how she had achieved all of it, until we had an eyewitness criminal turn on her and become an informant. There was a huge worldwide mob, a huge group of porn movie makers, who helped her. She supplied them with young virgin women and they then made movies using her computer knowledge to change the faces and other body parts after shooting the movie live."

The police officers remained quiet for a while as then the police chief said, "This is a worldwide problem where children, young girls, women, and even men are victims of kidnapping, rape, and murder schemes. Usually a missing woman or girl is reported and the victims are never found. One person fell in love with a prostitute and became our informant as he also found out she had died accidentally. His suspicion checked out to actually crack some parts of this case. Ms. Aideen made millions of dollars with this scheme and bought all of the hotels as a cover-up for her crimes. Yet Antonius van Phillip, Jacobus Vrederic van Phillip, and your brother Andries van Phillip with the help and support from the whole Kasteel Vrederic family have solved this case."

He kept on staring at the lighthouse as we all saw there was nothing in the lighthouse except the glowing lanterns.

He then said, "It was the evidence found in the cellar and the phone recordings of the criminal herself that have put everything together. Furthermore our hardest part was proving her artwork was not actually painted by hand but forged to look like hand-painted portraits. Cracking this puzzle helped put all of this to rest. It was a case that would have remained within the pages of unsolved mysteries without this family's help. We would like to thank the residents of Kasteel Vrederic on behalf of all the family members of the victims. At least now, all of them have closure."

The police had left and so had all the hidden burdens that had clouded our home. Big Mama was smiling again as I knew she was planning for the arrival of Andries. She never let go of her faith as I knew he too would rip the skies and the Earth apart to be born in her household over and over again.

Later in the evening as everyone finally returned to their own quarters, I heard footsteps come slowly toward my room as I saw a young woman stand at my door with eyes wide open.

I had for the first time asked her, "You can't sleep Katelijne? For I thought you had always slept so peacefully in my dreams. I would ask you to wake up yet you would just sleep. I wondered how were you sleeping when I was wide awake waiting for you."

She ran into my room and hugged me. It was a surprise I did not expect. Yet it really felt good to have her in my arms. All the untold tales of a lover's mind needed to be told. I knew I had so many nights of sweet dreams I had to share with her.

I asked her, "Mystical Princess, why does it seem like I know you so well, and we have been living as husband and wife for a long time? You know what I mean I hope."

She said, "I have so many nights of dreams I have seen with you, with our son, with this family I must share with you. No it's not strange as I know you better than I know my own self. I keep on wondering should I talk and let the night go to waste or sleep within your arms and not let a single night pass us by? Promise me you will never sleep on a different bed than me. Also promise me you will always wait for me to fall asleep as I get scared when I have to stay awake and can't sleep. Also promise me you will not die and leave me alone."

I watched the woman I barely knew yet I have known her all my life in my dreams as we had made love in our dreams so many times. I wondered how would she take it or was it even safe? How could I ask her?

She said, "Big Mama said not to sleep separately from you as we had spent too many nights just dreaming. She has arranged for our wedding to be in a few days."

I asked her then, "Miss Katelijne Snaaijer, will you marry me and become Mrs. Katelijne Snaaijer van Phillip, and eternally be mine?"

She smiled so sweetly as she kissed me on the lips and said, "I already am yours infinitely. Promise me you will always be only mine, as I am only yours. Also keep me hidden within your chest eternally and forever my beloved. Remember me eternally."

Dear Mrs. Katelijne Snaaijer van Phillip, this is my tenth poem for you. I give this one to you my beloved as now I can call you my wife.

REMEMBER ME ETERNALLY

Throughout the cold winter nights,
Hide inside my chest, my beloved wife.
During the summer's scorching heat
Be my sweet passion
And keep me within yourself.
If life gets harder than usual,
Be my peace and blessings.

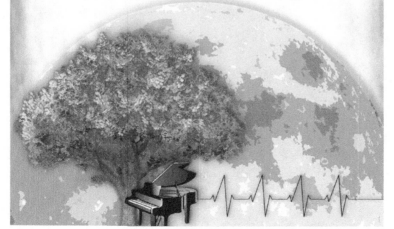

If I get lost and stranded,
Be my walking cane
And never let go of my hands.
When my home is dark and windy,
Be my lantern
And keep our lanterns
Safe from the heavy winds.
Never let go of our love
As I will always hold on to you
Through the bridge of love.
My beloved, my love, my wife,
Lovingly make our nights
A symbol of passion,

And if we are to stay awake
Throughout the nights,
May they be filled
With love potion
And wild passion
Uniting two souls into one.
My beloved,
During the day
While I am away,
Know I will definitely
Before night falls,
Reach our home.
Until then,

Keep the memories
Of our passionate night alive
And through them,

REMEMBER ME ETERNALLY.

Signed: Antonius van Phillip

CHAPTER TEN:

Conclusion Chapter: Heart Beats Your Name: Vows From The Beyond

"Twin flames' hearts beat for one another, a father's heart beats his children's name, a mother's heart beats her children's name, grandparents' hearts beat their grandchildren's name, yet in this story as well as all of the above, in his living Big Mama's name, a dead son's Heart Beats Your Name: Vows From The Beyond."

The van Phillip family united through the doors of dreams, reincarnation, and the musical sound of magical heartbeats.

Life at Kasteel Vrederic was joyous. It was a happy day as it was Christmas morning. Two years ago we had a few dark Christmases where there was no tree, and no one cooked nor were any presents in the house. Our home had lost the Christmas spirit. Yet today we had eggnog, Christmas cookies, Christmas puddings, Christmas pies, Dutch banketstaaf, Indian laddus, and fruit cakes displayed around the house. Our house smelled like an Indian kitchen, an American kitchen, and a typical Dutch kitchen. Gifts were left under the huge Christmas tree which Big Papa, Jacobus, and I with certain little hands had brought in.

Big Mama got back her sparks about seven months ago when like a miracle from the beyond, a new heart transplant survivor and a complete eye transplant survivor gave birth to our son. Heart transplant receivers normally are expected to live only for a few decades. Yet my wife is expected to live a complete healthy life without any complications. The medical scholars are calling this the miracle of Dr. Jacobus Vrederic van Phillip's magical hands. I know I too am a miracle survivor of my brother's magical hands as I could see my family during Christmas.

I knew my mother was busy with our baby boy who refused to leave Big Mama even for a minute. Katelijne actually loves how the grandson and grandmother are so close. She became Big Mama's daughter rather than daughter-in-law. Our son is Big Mama's heartbeat.

It was a very musical night when I saw my seven-month-old baby boy started to cry loudly and grab the whole household's attention. Jacobus came running as did Big Papa and Katelijne. I saw Ghileyn, Katelijne's father, too run in with gifts as he got scared why his grandson was crying.

Amidst all the chaos, we heard banging and screaming of two elderly women. One speaking in her native Hindi and the other in American English, came gushing in like a cyclone. Everyone pretty much knew they were threatening whoever harmed their baby boy will get cursed eternally by these two women. I was worried should I try to find out what happened to our son or make sure my great-grandmothers don't hurt themselves in the meanwhile.

Then we all watched our son say his first sentence as he cried out loud and said, "Big Mama, Andries van Phillip back as grandson. I keep my vows, my heart beats Big Mama."

Big Mama walked in and took him in her chest and listened to his magical heartbeats. She said, "My heart beats my three boys."

Destined to destiny is a path I don't believe in. I believe one must take control of his destiny as he foresees the end. Change it or try to escape it through changing the destination. As on that one frightful night, a storm came from nowhere and changed all of our preplanned travel destinations. Andries, Katelijne, and I, all three of us would have left this Earth. Yet through the blessed hands of a blessed son, a blessed brother, and a blessed doctor who had begun our family diaries, through his devotion kept our names alive in the pages of the diaries of Kasteel Vrederic.

All three of us survived. Yes, all three as two through the gifts of a donor who did not sacrifice his love but lived through and for his love. His love did not go in vain as a more powerful strength and belief than any love, a mother's love brought him back.

A mother's love crossed the door of death and brought back her son. For on that night and even afterward, a mother, Big Mama, through her belief in reincarnation and dreams, and her strong bond beyond the bond of blood, had called her son back to her. He too proved his love for his mother brought him back crossing even death for he proved a mother is not defined through giving birth but through love. All of the family members of Kasteel Vrederic held on to one another eternally as we said to one another, "Heart beats your name, vows from the beyond."

Our young child, my reincarnated brother, shocked everyone on this miraculous night. A child of seven months who could only say one or two words at a time, had been very clear as he called Big Mama by "Big Mama" not "Oma" as we tried to teach him. He would look at us like a magical singing bird and say, "Not Oma, Big Mama!"

He refused to go to anyone as he would jump to Big Mama and say, "My heart beats your name, vows from the beyond."

We all had a merry Christmas as time is a magical wagon where one day, the dark skies keep getting dark, yet on other days, dawn breaks through before the darkness even has a chance to evolve completely.

That night, however, I noticed my big brother Jacobus looked very tired as if he was in a trance of some kind. I asked Big Mama and Big Papa to come with me and ask him if everything was all right. We walked into his study where the original diarist, Jacobus van Vrederic, had written his famous diaries.

All the family members have ever since left their diaries in this library for the future generations to be guided by. The room was lighted and all the windows were closed as the drapes were left open. Wood logs were burning in the open hearth of the stone fireplace that was originally built by the famous diarist.

Big Papa asked Jacobus, "Son, what is the problem? You seem upset tonight."

Jacobus said, "Papa, something is wrong with Rietje, my granddaughter, from my previous life. I kept on hearing the same phrase, 'Opa's heart beats Rietje.' So, I entered the room and started to read her diary. I know you had read it as well as Big Mama. Tonight, however, I see the first few pages are here, when she met Alexander the knight in front of the Lover's Lighthouse. She was happy I had given her a diary to write in and start her own story. It has a few pages about the war but then the pages have become blank. Every day, the diary is becoming more and more blank."

Big Mama spoke at that and said, "I had a dream Rietje was captured and has been imprisoned. She was injured and needs help right away. She was calling her Opa for help. I believe Jacobus was injured too and was not able to travel. I heard them cry for one another. Then I saw Alexander the knight pray in front of the Lover's Lighthouse to the future generation for help."

It was then Jacobus told us, "I had the same dream Mama, and I don't know what to do. How can I help her if she is in the past and I am in the future?"

It was Big Papa who then said, "We are all in the same place. Even though they are in the past, we are in the future. So there must be a way to make a bridge and help. Anadhi, do you know a way?"

Big Mama said, "Yes, I do. In my dreams, I had traveled time to the past during various floods and wars. I guided others out of the events through my knowledge of the future events. So I know you can do it too. Remember my son, we travel to the future through the door of reincarnation. We can travel to the past through the door of dreams."

I did know what my mother was talking about. I only worried for the only brother I had left in this world. I watched my son and thought to myself I need a big brother too little one. The thought of the brother I loved more than my own life would be dream traveling by himself, worried me.

I knew he would not ever worry for himself for if there was ever anyone in need, then he forgets he even exists. The needs of all the other people in this world come before his own needs, and this was Rietje, the only ancestor we all came from. I wondered if there was any way I could dream travel to a place I never was with him. But I did not voice my thoughts. Nevertheless I knew I would never let him go alone.

Big Mama continued, "Still someone must sit here with you while you are traveling time through the tunnel of dreams. As a dream psychic, I know people travel time yet at times what you are going through in your dream, you can feel over here and it can be harmful. So, I will sit here next to you to make sure I don't lose another son. Also remember if you do travel, then the Margriete you had fallen in love with and still wait for to this day, is there but not yours for she belongs to the past Jacobus."

Jacobus laughed and said, "Dear Mother, I love her more than life, but I am an honorable noble man. Also, it's only a dream."

Big Papa said, "Yes, it was only a dream where I found my Anadhi in, yet I converted the dream to reality as I married her eternally."

Jacobus laughed and said, "Then I know I must come back honorable as my Margriete awaits my arrival in the twenty-first century, within the diaries of *Vows From The Beyond*. Yet I must now travel back in time to the seventeenth century and within the diaries of *I Shall Never Let You Go*.

I watched my family with my son in my arms. I knew my brother had traveled through the door of reincarnation to become my son and Big Mama's grandson. The horrific murders of the innocent women had left a permanent scar on the souls of those who have any. Yet the lessons of love and the power of true love and lovers should never be ignored. For where there is love, there is a way.

Deep within the heavenly skies or upon the Earth beneath, a bridge can be made through eternal, infinite lovers. All the twin flames who believe in love are throughout time watching over all the newborn twin flames. For just watch above the skies and upon the Earth, there is a bridge created through the blessed wings of twin flames. So if you are an eternal, infinite, immortal twin flame, then you too will be all right as you will find miraculous helping hands guiding you throughout time. Remember all you have to say is,

HEART BEATS YOUR NAME:
VOWS FROM THE BEYOND.

For all of you reading my diary tonight,

I have written this poem for you to recite

to your beloved tonight, tomorrow night,

and eternally forever after.

HEART BEATS YOUR NAME: VOWS FROM THE BEYOND

My beloved, my love,

If you can't find me,

Then touch your heart.

Listen to your inner feelings

For they will give you my messages.

I have never left you as long as

You keep me alive within your heart.

I am within your mind, body, and soul

As you know we are not two but one.

Let the tears roll for they will create

A reflecting pond where you will see me.

Let my memories flood you

With our sweet dreams

Of the magical nights.

Remember, I am always with you

As you are always with me.

My beloved,

My love,

My darling,

Remember, forever for you,

My,

HEART BEATS YOUR NAME:
VOWS FROM THE BEYOND.

I am Antonius van Phillip

and this is my diary.

PERSONAL LETTER
FROM THE AUTHOR

Dear beloved readers of the Kasteel Vrederic family,

I hope you all had a wonderful journey through the *Vows From The Beyond* diaries. Reawaken with belief and faith in true love. Remember when and where there is nothing, love still survives. All you have to do is believe in love. I know you all walked from the sixteenth century to the twenty-first century to meet and greet the future members of the Kasteel Vrederic family.

Now, however, we must go back to the seventeenth century and help save our beloved granddaughter Rietje. The only way to save her is to travel time to the *Vows From The Beyond* diaries and take back the expert, Dr. Jacobus Vrederic van Phillip. With his magical hands and with the help of modern science, he can save his lineage by traveling back in time to the seventeenth century through the *I Shall Never Let You Go* diaries.

Find out as Dr. Jacobus Vrederic van Phillip travels back in time to see himself as Jacobus van Vrederic, the famous diarist of the sixteenth and seventeenth-century *I Shall Never Let You Go* diaries, in *Entranced Beloved: I*

228

Shall Never Let You Go. Rietje and Alexander's eternal love story must be completed for the existence of all the inhabitants of *Vows From The Beyond*.

Happy reading everyone and keep an eye out for the crossover diary of *I Shall Never Let You Go* and *Vows From The Beyond* in the *Kasteel Vrederic* series, *Entranced Beloved: I Shall Never Let You Go*.

Now let us travel through the personal diaries of the inhabitants of Kasteel Vrederic. Original copies of these diaries are, however, kept with love and care in the blessed library of Kasteel Vrederic. For you though, here is a short glimpse into the complete series in order of reading.

BOOK ONE:

Eternally Beloved: I Shall Never Let You Go

This book introduces you to Kasteel Vrederic through the first diary of the famous diarist Jacobus van Vrederic. He walks you through his sad love story and goes through the love story of his daughter Griet van Jacobus and the brave soldier Theunis Peter. Based during the Dutch Eighty Years' War in the sixteenth century.

BOOK TWO:

Evermore Beloved: I Shall Never Let You Go
Here you walk through the amazing love
story of Jacobus van Vrederic and his
beloved wife Margriete van Wijck, where we
get to meet Jacobus's beloved granddaughter,
baby Rietje. Based during the witch trials and
the Dutch Eighty Years' War in the sixteenth
and seventeenth centuries.

BOOK THREE:

Be My Destiny: Vows From The Beyond.
This book takes you through reincarnation
and the blessed door of dreams. Here infinite
twin flames Erasmus van Phillip, a twenty-
first century descendant of Jacobus van
Vrederic and the reincarnated father of
Jacobus van Vrederic, is reborn again to find
and unite with his forever twin flame, Anadhi
Newhouse, also the reincarnated mother of
Jacobus van Vrederic. Find out how their son
reunites them through the twenty-first
century and takes them back to Kasteel
Vrederic.

BOOK FOUR:

Heart Beats Your Name: Vows From The Beyond

Here you will get introduced to a blind son of the Kasteel Vrederic family, the nephew and adopted son of Erasmus van Phillip and Anadhi Newhouse van Phillip. In this paranormal thriller, you will see how Dr. Jacobus Vrederic van Phillip, the biological son of Erasmus and Anadhi, guides his brother to unite with his pronounced dead wife, while trying to solve her murder mystery. A paranormal book where everyone realizes family members are bound with one another throughout time.

BOOK FIVE:

Entranced Beloved: I Shall Never Let You Go

Twenty-first century Dr. Jacobus Vrederic van Phillip must return to the seventeenth-century Kasteel Vrederic, as he realizes his beloved granddaughter is missing and must be rescued for the inhabitants of *Vows From The Beyond* to even exist. This can only be done through the miraculous hands of the famous twenty-first century physician. So here we go, Dr. Jacobus must travel time and go back to the *I Shall Never Let You Go* diaries. Walk back and get reacquainted with the seventeenth-century Kasteel Vrederic family members with Dr. Jacobus as he meets his sixteenth-century self, Jacobus van Vrederic. Margriete "Rietje" Jacobus Peters and Sir Alexander van der Bijl's love story is written and retold by the twenty-first century famous physician, Dr. Jacobus from the *Vows From The Beyond* diaries.

-Ann Marie Ruby

THE INHABITANTS OF
HEART BEATS YOUR NAME

Antonius van Phillip Son of Petrus van Phillip and Giada Berlusconi van Phillip, nephew and adopted son of Erasmus van Phillip and Anadhi Newhouse van Phillip, twin brother of Andries van Phillip, cousin and adopted brother of Jacobus Vrederic van Phillip, and twin flame and husband of Katelijne Snaaijer

Jacobus Vrederic van Phillip Son of Erasmus van Phillip and Anadhi Newhouse van Phillip, cousin of Antonius van Phillip and Andries van Phillip, and reincarnated form of sixteenth-century famous diarist Jacobus van Vrederic of the *I Shall Never Let You Go* diaries

Andries van Phillip Son of Petrus van Phillip and Giada Berlusconi van Phillip, nephew and adopted son of Erasmus van Phillip and Anadhi Newhouse van Phillip, twin brother of Antonius van Phillip, cousin and adopted brother of Jacobus Vrederic van Phillip, and deceased yet reincarnated as son

of Antonius van Phillip and
Katelijne Snaaijer

Erasmus van
Phillip
World-renowned painter, twenty-first-century owner of Kasteel Vrederic, son of Greta van Phillip, descendant of the van Vrederic family, husband of Anadhi Newhouse van Phillip, father of Jacobus Vrederic van Phillip, uncle and adopted father of Antonius van Phillip and Andries van Phillip, and reincarnated form of sixteenth-century Johannes van Vrederic

Anadhi Newhouse
van Phillip
Author, daughter of Dr. Andrew Newhouse and Dr. Gita Shankar Newhouse, granddaughter of Martin Newhouse and Miranda Newhouse, granddaughter of Hari Shankar and Parvati Shankar, wife of Erasmus van Phillip, mother of Jacobus Vrederic van Phillip, aunt and adopted mother of Antonius van Phillip and Andries van Phillip, and reincarnated form of sixteenth-century Mahalt

Katelijne Snaaijer
Twin flame and wife of Antonius van Phillip, mother of reincarnated form of Andries van Phillip, and stepdaughter of Ghileyn Snaaijer

Josquin de Cloet Best friend of Antonius van Phillip

Livina Bakker-Beenhouwer Owner of Mirrorless Hotel, wife of Luyt Bakker, and adopted mother of Aideen Bakker

Luyt Bakker Owner of Mirrorless Hotel, husband of Livina Bakker-Beenhouwer, and adopted father of Aideen Bakker

Aideen Bakker Daughter of owners Livina Bakker-Beenhouwer and Luyt Bakker of Mirrorless Hotel

Ghileyn Snaaijer Husband of Jantje Snaaijer, Stepfather of Katelijne Snaaijer, and Protestant preacher

Jantje Snaaijer Wife of Ghileyn Snaaijer, and mother of Katelijne Snaaijer, deceased

Egisrico Beekhof Church caretaker

Aunt Marinda Psychic, tarot card reader, spiritual seer, and descendant of sixteenth and seventeenth-century Aunt Marinda from the *I Shall Never Let You Go* diaries

Miranda Newhouse "Grandmother" Seeker, paternal grandmother of Anadhi Newhouse van Phillip, mother of Dr. Andrew Newhouse, wife of Martin Newhouse, descendant of Bertelmeeus van der Berg from the *I Shall Never Let You Go* diaries, and great-grandmother of Jacobus Vrederic van Phillip

Parvati Shankar "Nani" Maternal grandmother of Anadhi Newhouse van Phillip, mother of Dr. Gita Shankar Newhouse, wife of Hari Shankar, and great-grandmother of Jacobus Vrederic van Phillip

Greta van Phillip Mother of Erasmus van Phillip and descendant of van Vrederic family, deceased

Griete van Phillip Aunt of Erasmus van Phillip and descendant of van Vrederic family, deceased

Grietje van Phillip Aunt of Erasmus van Phillip and descendant of van Vrederic family, deceased

Matthias van Phillip Cousin of Erasmus van Phillip, lives in New Delhi, India

Petrus van Phillip Cousin of Erasmus van Phillip, husband of Giada Berlusconi van Phillip, and father of twins Antonius van Phillip and Andries van Phillip, deceased

Giada Berlusconi van Phillip Wife of Petrus van Phillip, and mother of twins Antonius van

Phillip and Andries van Phillip, deceased

Jacobus van Vrederic   Sixteenth and seventeenth-century owner of Kasteel Vrederic, Protestant preacher, son of Johannes van Vrederic and Mahalt, husband of Margriete van Wijck, father of Griet van Jacobus, grandfather of Margriete "Rietje" Jacobus Peters, and the diarist of the *I Shall Never Let You Go* diaries

Margriete van Wijck   Sixteenth and seventeenth-century inhabitant, beloved wife of Jacobus van Vrederic, mother of Griet van Jacobus, and grandmother of Margriete "Rietje" Jacobus Peters from the *I Shall Never Let You Go* diaries

Theunis Peters   Sixteenth-century inhabitant, honorable soldier, husband of Griet van Jacobus, father of Margriete "Rietje" Jacobus Peters, son-in-law of Jacobus van Vrederic and Margriete van Wijck from the *I Shall Never Let You Go* diaries, and spirit of Kasteel Vrederic

Griet van Jacobus   Sixteenth-century inhabitant, daughter of Jacobus van Vrederic and Margriete van Wijck, wife of Theunis Peters, mother of Margriete "Rietje" Jacobus Peters from the *I Shall Never Let You Go* diaries, and spirit of Kasteel Vrederic

Margriete "Rietje" Jacobus Peters   Sixteenth and seventeenth-century inhabitant, seventeenth-century owner of Kasteel Vrederic, granddaughter of Jacobus van Vrederic and Margriete van Wijck, daughter of Theunis Peters and Griet van Jacobus, wife of Sir Alexander van der Bijl, and inheritor and co-diarist of the fifth diary in the *Kasteel Vrederic* series

Sir Alexander van der Bijl   Sixteenth and seventeenth-century inhabitant, great-grandnephew of Sir Krijn van der Bijl, and husband of Margriete "Rietje" Jacobus Peters from the *I Shall Never Let You Go* diaries

Johannes van Vrederic   Sixteenth-century inhabitant, original owner of Kasteel Vrederic, husband of Mahalt, and father of Jacobus van Vrederic, from the *I Shall Never Let You Go* diaries

Mahalt   Sixteenth-century inhabitant, wife of Johannes van Vrederic, and mother of Jacobus van Vrederic

GLOSSARY

Get acquainted with some Dutch and Hindi terms, and places in the Netherlands, India, and the United States that were used in this book.

Aloo Matar	Potatoes and peas, usually cooked in a curry style
Amsterdam	Capital city of the Netherlands
Amsterdam Airport Schiphol	One of the busiest airports in the world and main international airport in the Netherlands
Appelstroop	Apple syrup
Banketstaaf	Dutch puff pastry
Brussels	Capital city of Belgium
Chattanooga	City in the state of Tennessee
Dam Square	Historic square in Amsterdam, the Netherlands
Den Haag	The Hague, political capital city of the Netherlands within the province of South Holland

Dokkum Town in the province of Friesland in the Netherlands

Dolly Parton World-renowned American singer, movie star, and artist from the state of Tennessee

Dollywood Theme park in Tennessee co-owned by Dolly Parton and Herschend Family Entertainment

Dutch Term refers to both the language spoken and the people in the Netherlands

Dutch Golden Age Time period from 1588 to 1672 when the Dutch were world-renowned for their trade, art, science, and more

Eindhoven City in the province of North Brabant in the Netherlands

Elvis Presley World-renowned American singer, movie star, and artist, lived in the famous Graceland Mansion in Memphis, Tennessee

Friesland Province located in the northern Netherlands

Gatlinburg City in the state of Tennessee, bordering the Great Smoky Mountains National Park, also

	known as the Gateway to the Great Smoky Mountains
Grachtengordel	Canal Ring consists of the four main canals of Amsterdam, the Netherlands, declared as a UNESCO World Heritage Site in 2013
Great Smoky Mountains	Famous mountain range that extends through Tennessee and North Carolina, also known as the Smokies
Groningen	Province located in the northeastern Netherlands
Hagelslag	Sprinkles used as topping for buttered bread
Herengracht	Patricians' Canal, one of the main canals in Amsterdam, the Netherlands
Hindi	Language spoken in India, one of the official languages of the Indian government
India	Officially the Republic of India, country located in South Asia, and the second most populated country in the world
Kasteel Vrederic	Castle Vrederic is the home of the van Vrederic family in the *Kasteel Vrederic* series,

spanning from the sixteenth century through the present

Keizersgracht Emperor's Canal, one of the main canals in Amsterdam, the Netherlands

Laddu Typical Indian dessert, various types

Loppersum Village in the province of Groningen in the Netherlands

Memphis City in the state of Tennessee, home of Elvis Presley

Naarden City in the province of North Holland in the Netherlands

Nani Maternal grandmother in Hindi

Nashville Capital city of the state of Tennessee

New Delhi Capital of India

Noord-Brabant North Brabant, province located in the southern Netherlands

North Carolina State in southeastern United States of America, capital city is Raleigh

Oma Grandmother in Dutch

Opa Grandfather in Dutch

Paratha	Type of flatbread, similar to roti but made out of flour or wheat and fried, popular in Indian subcontinent
Prinsengracht	Prince's Canal, one of the main canals in Amsterdam, the Netherlands
Roti	Type of flatbread popular in Indian subcontinent
Sabzee	Mixed vegetable curry
Singel	Belt, one of the main canals in Amsterdam, the Netherlands
Tennessee	State in southeastern United States of America, capital city is Nashville
The Netherlands	Country in Western Europe, dreamland of Ann Marie Ruby
The United States of America	Country in North America, home of Ann Marie Ruby
White cane	An individual using a white cane while walking signifies the individual has no vision and is totally blind

MESSAGE FROM THE AUTHOR

"Messages left in the pages of a diary become treasured riches for all who get to open the sacred pages and grasp the message."

Dear Cherished Readers,

Messages left within a book travel time as they become cherished throughout time. An infinite love story can unite heavens above and Earth beneath if you only believe. Love becomes immortal when you the beloved find your beloved and know it is within this union, another set of twin flames are born.

I have heard stories that love does not exist and is only within books. Yet remember life is a journey through time. If you are still complaining about nonexistent love, then you should remember you still have hope.

In this book, my lead characters believed in the miracles of the beyond and let love be just love. My lead character sees the moon above the skies and knows he will write poems about the moon and how she is sleeping in the skies tonight. Then he imagines one day, his moon will come to him and sleep on his chest. On that day, he will write about her, yet tonight he still can dream about her.

My characters let the door of dreams take them to one another. For when and where there is faith and belief, love will follow, as you only need to follow your heartbeats. Love is like the singing nightingales, who keep on singing for one another. Love is like the rising phoenix where for one another, you rise from ashes.

My book also shows the bond and love found within a family. Soul families hold on to one another throughout time. Here you don't judge one another but have faith in one another. A brother has faith and love that pull him and guide him to honor, love, and protect his brother from all the obstacles of life, even death.

My book shows a mother's love for her children has no limitation or bound as a mother can hear and feel a child when the child calls her. Social awareness is a topic not often covered in romance fictions yet I know at this time and age with so much advanced technologies, we must not forget the evil side of this technological system we can't live without. We have all over the world, sex trafficking.

Children are gone missing every day. Parents living in fear of sex traffickers have all the citizens live with our doors closed, alarm systems installed, and night lights kept on in the porches during the night. However, if we could all become a human chain of helpers and protectors of one another, then honorable citizens like Andries van Phillip would still be alive.

He gave his life to save another life, and by doing so, he saved so many other lives. Yet a mother stays awake at night crying for her son. A brother wishes for him to still be here. A father waits for his son to return home. Yet all for what? So some cheap, low-class pornographic movie can be made at the expense of kidnapping a daughter, at the expense of demoralizing the society, at the expense of a few minutes of selfish pleasures of one.

These evil acts of the human minds can be prevented if you don't support them and don't let our sisters and brothers be a victim of unjust social crimes committed by the dark people hiding within the society. We can stop them if only we unite and let them know an honorable life is better than a life hiding in the cellar and creating a pornographic movie for sex trafficking. Let's say no to all of these unhealthy, dirty hidden crimes being committed in the cellars of a dirty society. Come on everyone, let's protect and bring back all the innocent victims of these crimes with honor, dignity, and love.

Even though this book is completely fictional and actually has no medical advice related to actual facts, my thought was what if a transplant survivor too could dream of being a hundred years old. In this book, my message is why not? I have a message for all organ transplant survivors and for all of you who wait for a miracle. My message is for you the mother who might have a child in need of a transplant and asks you will he or she live to be a hundred years old. Your answer should always be yes, you will.

There is always a miracle waiting for you too. Miracles are just that, miracles, where and when there is a believer waiting, for the believers are miracles from the beyond. Hope is the first miracle and all of you who believe in miracles are the path to the magical door of miracles happening every day. Believe in dawn and the sun will rise for you tomorrow.

Medical expenses globally have forced people to take on jobs they under normal circumstances would avoid or run in the opposite direction from. My character had no choice but to go for a job she would have avoided under normal circumstances. We, the society, must unitedly do something to reduce this cost to the human capability and capacity level. It's you who can make the difference if only you too love our one world and one human race as one family. You can try to help protect and be there for one another.

My message for all the children of this world is you are not an orphan or alone because I will always be there for you as well as people like my characters. The word "Mother" needs to be seen through Anadhi Newhouse van Phillip's eyes. Who says you have to give birth to be a mother? A mother takes birth through love, not by giving birth.

In this world, no child should feel lonely or call themselves an orphan or an adopted child. For the bond between a child and a mother can never be broken through birth or death. It's eternal.

I would ask all of you to talk with one another and ask each other for help. Ask your parents for guidance. Go and talk with your beloved. Always see one another through the loving eyes of twin flames, through the loving eyes of a soul family, through the loving eyes of a mother, and through the loving eyes of a father. You the reader try to see this through my eyes.

Where there is an obstacle, there is always a way out. The family members of Kasteel Vrederic would say, follow your heartbeats, they will never lie. In conclusion, I would like to say,

Heart Beats Your Name: Vows From The Beyond.

ABOUT THE AUTHOR

"Meet Ann Marie Ruby from Seattle, Washington.
This is her story."

Ann Marie Ruby was born into a diplomatic family for which she had the privilege of traveling the world. This upbringing made the whole world her one family. She never saw a country as a foreign country yet as a neighbor who was there for her as she would be there for them. After all, isn't that what families do for one another?

Ann Marie became an author as she started to place her chosen words into the pages of her diaries. She knew she must collect all her thoughts and produce them into different diaries. Each diary became her different books.

Ann Marie's life goal is not to just write something but only what she believes in. So all her thoughts and words remained within the pages of her diaries until she realized it was time she must share them with you. Otherwise, she felt selfish and knew that was not her characteristic as she lives for everyone, not just for herself.

INTERNATIONAL #1 BESTSELLING AUTHOR:

Ann Marie became an international number-one bestselling author of seventeen books. Alongside being a full-time author, she loves to write articles on her website where she can have a better connection with all of you. Ann Marie, a dream psychic, became a blogger and a humanitarian only because she believes in you and herself as a complete, honest, and open family.

PERSONAL:

Ann Marie is an American who grew up in Brisbane, Australia. She resided in the Washington, D.C. area, but later settled in Seattle, Washington. In her spare time when she is not writing books, she loves to meditate, pray, listen to music, cook, and write blog posts.

BESTSELLING:

Ann Marie's books have placed her on top 100 bestselling charts in various countries including the Netherlands, United States, United Kingdom, Canada, and Germany. In 2020, she became a household name as her books began to consistently rank #1 on multiple bestselling charts. *The Netherlands: Land Of My Dreams* and *Everblooming: Through The Twelve Provinces Of The Netherlands*, both became overnight number-one bestsellers in the United States.

In 2020, *The Netherlands: Land Of My Dreams* also became a bestseller in the Netherlands and Canada, consistently becoming #1 on various lists and one of the top selling books on Amazon NL. *Everblooming: Through The Twelve Provinces Of The Netherlands* became #37 on the Netherlands top 100 bestselling Amazon books chart which includes all books from all genres. Ann Marie's other books have also made various top 100 bestselling lists and received multiple accolades including *Eternal Truth: The Tunnel Of Light* which was named as one of eight thought-provoking books by women.

ROMANCE FICTION:

Ann Marie's *Kasteel Vrederic* series was written in a diary fashion. She has always kept a diary herself, so she thought her characters too could keep a diary. All of their diaries became individual books yet collectively, they are a part of a family, the Kasteel Vrederic family.

OTHER BOOKS:

All of Ann Marie's nonfiction and fiction books are available globally. You can take a look at short descriptions about the books at the end of this book.

THE NETHERLANDS:

Ann Marie revealed why many of her books revolve around the Netherlands, sharing that as a dream psychic, she had seen the historical past of a country in her dreams and was later able to place a name to the country. This is described in detail in *Spiritual Lighthouse: The Dream Diaries Of Ann Marie Ruby* and *The Netherlands: Land Of My Dreams* where she also wrote about her plans to eventually move to the Netherlands.

Ann Marie has received letters on behalf of His Majesty King Willem-Alexander and Her Majesty Queen Máxima of the Netherlands after they received her books *The Netherlands: Land Of My Dreams* and *Everblooming: Through The Twelve Provinces Of The Netherlands*. Additionally, Ann Marie has received letters on behalf of His Excellency Mark Rutte, the Prime Minister of the Netherlands for her books.

WRITING:

Ann Marie also is acclaimed globally as one of the top voices in the spiritual space, however, she is recognized for her writing abilities published across many genres namely spirituality, lifestyle, inspirational quotations, poetry, fiction, romance, history, travel, social awareness, and more. Her writing style is hailed by critics and readers alike as making readers feel as though they have made a friend.

FOLLOW THE AUTHOR:

Now as you have found her book, why don't you and Ann Marie become friends? Join her and become a part of her global family. Ann Marie shall always give you books which you will read and then find yourself as a part of her book family.

For more information about Ann Marie Ruby, any one of her books, or to read her blog posts and articles, subscribe to her website, www.annmarieruby.com.

Follow Ann Marie Ruby on social media:
Twitter: @AnnahMariahRuby
Facebook: @TheAnnMarieRuby
Instagram: @Ann_Marie_Ruby
Pinterest: @TheAnnMarieRuby

BOOKS BY THE AUTHOR

INSPIRATIONAL QUOTATIONS SERIES:

This series includes four books of original quotations and one omnibus edition.

Spiritual Travelers:
Life's Journey From The Past
To The Present
For The Future

Spiritual
Messages:
From A Bottle

Spiritual Journey:
Life's Eternal Blessings

Spiritual
Inspirations:
Sacred Words
Of Wisdom

Omnibus edition contains all four books of original quotations.

Spiritual Ark:
The Enchanted Journey Of Timeless
Quotations

SPIRITUAL SONGS SERIES:

This series includes two original spiritual prayer books.

SPIRITUAL SONGS: LETTERS FROM MY CHEST

When there was no hope, I found hope within these sacred words of prayers, I but call songs. Within this book, I have for you, 100 very sacred prayers.

SPIRITUAL SONGS II: BLESSINGS FROM A SACRED SOUL

Prayers are but the sacred doors to an individual's enlightenment. This book has 123 prayers for all humans with humanity.

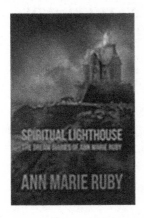

SPIRITUAL LIGHTHOUSE: THE DREAM DIARIES OF ANN MARIE RUBY

Do you believe in dreams? For within each individual dream, there is a hidden message and a miracle interlinked. Learn the spiritual, scientific, religious, and philosophical aspects of dreams. Walk with me as you travel through forty nights, through the pages of my book.

THE WORLD HATE CRISIS: THROUGH THE EYES OF A DREAM PSYCHIC

Humans have walked into an age where humanity now is being questioned as hate crimes have reached a catastrophic amount. Let us in union stop this crisis. Pick up my book and see if you too could join me in this fight.

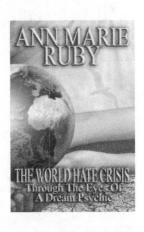

ETERNAL TRUTH: THE TUNNEL OF LIGHT

Within this book, travel with me through the doors of birth, death, reincarnation, true soulmates and twin flames, dreams, miracles, and the end of time.

THE NETHERLANDS: LAND OF MY DREAMS

Oh the sacred travelers, be like the mystical river and journey through this blessed land through my book. Be the flying bird of wisdom and learn about a land I call, Heaven on Earth.

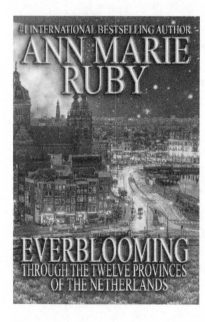

EVERBLOOMING: THROUGH THE TWELVE PROVINCES OF THE NETHERLANDS

Original poetry and hand-picked tales are bound together in this keepsake book. Come travel with me as I take you through the lives of the Dutch past.

LOVE LETTERS: THE TIMELESS TREASURE

Fifty original timeless treasured love poems are presented with individual illustrations describing each poem.

KASTEEL VREDERIC SERIES:

ETERNALLY BELOVED: I SHALL NEVER LET YOU GO

Travel time to the sixteenth century where Jacobus van Vrederic, a beloved lover and father, surmounts time and tide to find the vanished love of his life. On his pursuit, Jacobus discovers secrets that will alter his life evermore. He travels through the Eighty Years' War-ravaged country, the Netherlands as he takes the vow, even if separated by a breath, "Eternally beloved, I shall never let you go."

EVERMORE BELOVED: I SHALL NEVER LET YOU GO

Jacobus van Vrederic returns with the devoted spirits of Kasteel Vrederic. A knight and a seer also join him on a quest to find his lost evermore beloved. They journey through a war-ravaged country, the Netherlands, to stop another war which was brewing silently in his land, called the witch hunts. Time was his enemy as he must defeat time and tide to find his evermore beloved wife alive.

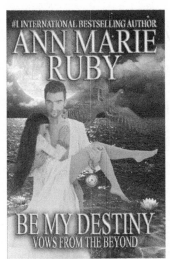

BE MY DESTINY: VOWS FROM THE BEYOND

Fighting their biggest enemy destiny, twin flames Erasmus van Phillip and Anadhi Newhouse are reborn over and over again only to lose the battle to destiny. Find out if through the helping hands of sacred spirits of the sixteenth century, these eternal twin flames are finally able to unite in the twenty-first century, as they say, "Reincarnation is a blessing if only you are mine."

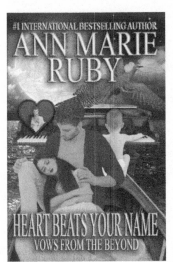

HEART BEATS YOUR NAME: VOWS FROM THE BEYOND

While one is sleepless, the other twin flame is sleeping eternally. Now how does Antonius van Phillip awaken his twin flame Katelijne Snaaijer from beyond Earth, and solve a murder mystery, she is the only witness to yet also a victim of? Find out how the musical sound of heartbeats guide him to his sleeping beloved while he solves the mystery sleepless.

Coming Soon

**ENTRANCED BELOVED:
I SHALL NEVER
LET YOU GO**

ENTRANCED BELOVED: I SHALL NEVER LET YOU GO

The fifth book in this series is coming soon.

Coming Soon

FORBIDDEN DAUGHTER OF KASTEEL VREDERIC: VOWS FROM THE BEYOND

FORBIDDEN DAUGHTER OF KASTEEL VREDERIC: VOWS FROM THE BEYOND

The sixth book in this series is coming soon.

Made in the USA
Las Vegas, NV
28 December 2023

83643878R00163